Dear John

Yet you

D1050677

# Life on All Fours

A Novel

David A. Fredrickson

Love,

David and
(Rufus)

RUF Publishing
Life on All Fours: A Novel
David A. Fredrickson

Cover Design: Tim Simmons
Biography Photograph: Duane Cramer
Copyeditor: Gabriella West

Published in the United States by RUF Publishing
ISBN: 978-0-9908002-0-0

# Dedication

*Life on All Fours* is dedicated to Rufus, my best friend and muse. (July 4, 2002—June 17, 2014)

## This Little Light

Halley's Comet blazes across the sky
Too bright, too beautiful, gone too soon
Firecracker baby born on the Fourth of July
This little light of mine

Wiggle, wag, propeller tail, meant to soar
Red-brown beauty in motion, one speed—YES
Into cautious laps and hearts he flies
This little light of mine

Wonder and awe, with every pitter-patter
Paws that race to keep up with possibility
On a leash, at times tethered to reluctant feet
This little light of mine

"Yes you can," wet nose inches close and closer
Slow down, wait, too messy, too much
Undaunted, his kiss always as close as he can
This little light of mine

"Oh the places we can sniff, you and me—you'll see."
Not this time, stop pulling, leave it
He shakes it off, lets it go, forgives, next time …
This little light of mine

"Everywhere you are, I want to be."
The jingle of his tags like sacred chimes
Follows, bears witness, even as he snores
This little light of mine

How can this much life ever be dead?
Yet he leaves as he arrived
Too bright, too beautiful, gone too soon
This little light of mine

But in my tears is the warmth of his glow
His nose print forever on the window of my soul
Heart breaking yet full, this love has changed me
His little light IS mine

# Table of Contents

# Acknowledgements

Thank you to all who have shared their untold stories with me, whether in therapy, support groups, or spontaneous conversations. *Life on All Fours* is a reflection of our stories—stories that are often unheard because of shame and isolation. We can't change our story unless we know our story. And we can't truly know our story unless we tell it.

Thank you to my family and friends who have encouraged and loved me through this process. I am blessed to have such a wonderful and supportive community.

Thank you to the faithful readers of *The Rufus Chronicles*, the inspiration for this book. Your interest in Rufus's annual review gave me the courage to dig deeper.

Thank you to those who have read excepts and full drafts of *Life on All Fours*: Jörg Fockele, Dan Fredrickson, Becky Fredrickson, Gina Genovese, Susan Giba, Chuck Guice, Susie Hara, Ana Homayoun, Linda Mantel, Cindy McCarthy, Mytrae Meliana, Jay Odessky, Nina Raff, Roxane Ramos, Diane Sanchez, Gerda Schlacher, Eddie Sheehan, Tim Simmons, John Sinclair, Susi Stadler, Carrie Suriano, Jose Villegas, Gabriella West, and Annie Winters. I have been challenged and encouraged by your feedback. I am a better writer and this is a better book because of you.

Thank you Lakendra Fredrickson for our Weekly Meeting. I thought I was going to be the mentor but ended up being the mentee.

Thank you to my copyeditor, Gabriella West, and those who read this manuscript with an editor's eye. It's amazing what I missed and you discovered in your readings.

Thank you Duane Cramer for your amazing photography.

Thank you Tim Simmons for inspiring me to see the story in the book cover. I am indebted to your design skills and artistic eye.

Thank you to my writing group, Gina Genovese, Mytrae Meliana, and Gabriella West, who critiqued and celebrated *Life on all Fours* from its inception. My writing identity has been shaped by our shared experience. Thank you for your wisdom, dedication, and generosity.

# Life

## ON ALL FOURS

# Chapter 1

# Tails

I'm always losing things. And it's always the things I love the most that end up missing. I can't tell you how many balls I've lost, how many bones have gone hiding, and how many tug ropes have disappeared. It seems I spend all my time looking! But I'd have to say my biggest loss was my tail. Tails are hairy signs of "something good is going to happen" on a spring-loaded stick — the bigger the swish, the brighter the wish. Everyone should have a tail. It's hard to understand how I could have lost mine. All that's left is a stub. But then, I come from a family of stubs. Mama told me it's the way we're supposed to be.

I sometimes wonder what it would be like to have a full tail. What would it feel like to have a tail that swings through the air instead of just tapping in place? But I can't complain, my tail still works. In fact, it works harder than any tail you'll ever see. It doesn't start with a lazy thump-thump. It takes off with a zoom at the first sign of possibility. It always looks for adventure, the thrill of finding something that is better than anything I could have ever expected. My dad, Ben, never had a tail, not even a stub. But I'm getting ahead of myself.

My name is Beau, and my story begins on April 13, 1997, in a puppy pile. I remember being snuggled and cuddled by a wiggling, reddish-brown baby blanket made up of my brothers and one sister. There were five of us, all wrapped together in warm and cozy bliss. It was impossible to know what jiggling tail, moist cold nose, or silky ear was mine or belonged to someone else. All the pink, tender bellies and sweet puppy breath were one, connected by a memory that we remembered when we piled together next to Mama. Mama was big and liver colored. Her hair hung wavy from her belly and legs. She had big, floppy ears and a strong, wet nose that was constantly smelling and pushing us around. She often worked us over with her rough and slobbery tongue, and if we tried to get away she held us down with her heavy paw. In those early days, Mama stayed close . . . unless her human showed up. I remember the first time I met Joanne, nose to nose.

"Oh my, my, my, look at my lil' babies, ohhhh, my lil' lub bugs." Joanne's voice danced like butterflies.

We all wiggled and scooted toward the happy sounds. I looked up her long legs and realized that only two of her paws were on the ground. The other two were dangling by her side.

"Sadie, sweet pooch, oh, you did good! Your babies are beautiful." Her words drifted high above my head.

I wondered where were the smells? Where did the food go in? Where did it come out? I assumed all the interesting body parts were perched high in the sky. But no matter how high I stretched I couldn't get close enough.

"Oh, and look at this one. Aren't you something? Can I have a look, Sadie dear?" The voice moved closer.

Suddenly everything was within reach. I was sitting in the palm of Joanne's hand floating toward her face, my first human face. There was so much to explore. The scents were new and exciting. Her mouth was ripe, some smells near the surface and others buried deep inside. Her ears tasted warm and sour, her hair was oily and sweet.

"Oh, lil' chubby-tubby, such da sweetie. Look at you, with your two-toned coat, da wiggle worm," Joanne laughed.

I twisted and squirmed with excitement.

"Hold still, boo. Let me check you out."

Her fingers roamed everywhere. I started to relax with hands that felt like they belonged. Mama moved closer to Joanne and wagged her tail.

As we grew, we saw more of Joanne. Mama was different when Joanne was around. Mama would dance and skip like she had puppy paws. She couldn't wait to be with Joanne, away from us! Once she was on the other side of our pen she would roll over on her back and let Joanne rub her belly. Mama never gave her belly so easily to us.

We loved Mama's belly. It was loaded with the smells and tastes of Mama. The eating-room hung heavy—five suck knobs were attached to her smooth and droopy skin. Oh, the taste of Mama's milk! Warm juice marinated in subtle hints of sweet and tang. We sucked with sloppy grunts and moans as milk squirted over our tongues. However, our bliss was short lived because we soon discovered that there wasn't always enough. The suck knobs could unexpectedly go dry, or sometimes Mama would just get up with a huff and leave our smacking mouths sucking air. Feeding time changed us. I discovered a mean rumble in the back of my throat when it was time to eat. My brothers and sister became mouths that could make me go hungry. I learned that if you want it, take it. And if you want to keep it, show your teeth. Mealtime turned into snarling, snapping fights. Our razor-sharp teeth could pierce with unknowing speed. Danger constantly surrounded the softest part of Mama.

I remember the first time I bit Mama. I had found one of the good suck knobs and one of my brothers wanted my spot. I remember his hard head butting up against me as he growled in my ear and his mouth moved in for the steal. I did the only thing I could—I held on with my teeth. Well, Mama jumped up with such speed that all five balls of fuzz were sent into orbit, all flying in different directions. As we somersaulted and skidded across the floor, the room was filled with squeals and yelps. But our outrage quickly turned to fear. Mama was on all fours, glaring at all of us. Her lip curled above her teeth in a trembling snarl. Long white daggers glistened in the corners of her mouth as her eyes moved slowly from puppy to puppy. We all cowered and slowly backed away with our tails tucked and our bellies as close to the ground as possible. It seemed completely possible that one of us was going to get skewered. I don't know what would have happened if Joanne hadn't showed up.

"What the . . . SADIE, NO!" Joanne shouted in her big voice and rushed over to our puppy pen.

Joanne glared at Mama. "Sadie, shame on you, these are your babies!"

Mama hung her head. Joanne bent down and we all scampered toward her out-stretched hands. Her hands glided over our pudgy bodies as we jumped and whimpered, our tails flapping with relief. Mama stood silently and watched.

"What got into you, Sadie?" Joanne said more softly. "I know it's not easy." She sighed. "You poor dear, all these hungry mouths to feed."

Mama's tail began to bounce when Joanne's voice changed. Mama trotted over to Joanne and stuck her nose in Joanne's ear and licked.

"You're a good girl. I know you're doing your best. It'll get easier. Soon they'll be eating real food."

Joanne's hands abandoned us, leaving us exposed. Her hands found Mama and started to rub her ears. Human hands no longer protected our soft skin. We crouched, eyes focused on Mama.

"Come on, Sadie, you need a break." Joanne stood up. "Let's take a walk."

Mama quickly jumped over the fence. Her paws clicked and Joanne's feet padded across the hard floor, squeak, slam . . . then quiet. We all stood still, straining our ears and sniffing the air, no signs of Mama or Joanne. Alone, hungry but out of danger, we gave up our fight with each other and cuddled together.

Mama was changing. In the beginning her breaths were big and peaceful. Then her sighs turned into exhausted surrender and then grumbles and growls. She was spending more time away from the puppy pen. As we grew bigger, she grew more distant and weary. She began to watch us with a strange look in her eye while constantly looking outside of our pen, looking and waiting for something. Without Mama's constant attention, I spent more time with my brothers and sister. I discovered that I liked to be chased. When things got going, I was always first to turn and dart away with someone, or everyone, right on my heels. There's nothing like the heart-thumping feel of teeth almost on your heels, just out of reach.

We also spent more time out of our pen with Joanne. Our noses led our discoveries. Smells could stop us in our tracks or send us in a new direction, pulling in the world through our twitching noses. It was always a race to see who could get there first, and we didn't like to share.

I remember my first toy. Joanne was sitting on the floor and I was roaming the area around her when her hand grabbed me like soft teeth and rolled me on my back. I nipped at her fingers and tried to get back on my feet. Suddenly her other hand appeared with a soft fuzzy and she shook it in my face. It didn't have any eyes, and one of its ears was missing. It smelled familiar.

"This was your Mama's," Joanne chuckled.

Joanne threw it into the next room. A machine next to Joanne began to ring, but I ignored it and raced after Fuzzy.

"Hello," Joanne said into the talking-machine.

"This is Joanne Anderson."

I caught up with Fuzzy and clamped down with my teeth. He shouted back at me with a loud squeak. I jumped back and growled.

"Hi, Ben, yes, I've got puppies. There are five in the litter, four males and one bitch, and I need one more home for one of the males."

I crept back and nudged him with my nose but he didn't move.

"I'm very careful with breeding so my dogs are very healthy. I have a good reputation in the business and I also do the dog shows. In fact, the father of this litter is one of my champions."

"Usually Field Spaniels are liver or black, but the puppy that's available is tan and liver."

"They're four weeks old, born April 13."

"The puppies will be ready for homes at eight weeks."

I picked up Fuzzy with my teeth and he squeaked again, but this time I didn't let go. I shook him and he squeaked louder.

"Yeah, that's one of the puppies. Actually he's the one that still needs a home. He's such a cutie-pie. He just discovered that the stuffy toy talks," she laughed. "He's very special. I considered keeping him, but I just don't have the time right now to work with a puppy."

"Have you had a dog before?"

"What do you do for a living?"

"That should be good preparation. If you can teach teenagers, a puppy is going to be a cakewalk." Joanne smiled.

"When is your summer vacation?"

"That could be perfect timing. They'll be ready to travel the second week of June."

I jumped in Joanne's lap with Fuzzy and disappeared in the cave of her criss-crossed legs.

"You wouldn't need to come here. I'd send him to you. Where do you live?"

"It's no problem. I fly puppies all over the country. San Francisco would be an easy flight from Seattle."

Joanne started to gently rub my back.

"Send me an email and I'll send you some more information. There's an application you'll need to fill out. The sooner I hear back from you the better, because I have a couple other people who are interested. I'll send you some pictures. Be prepared to fall in love."

"OK. Talk to you soon."

"Bye."

I closed my eyes and settled into Joanne's lap with Fuzzy, my new friend.

# Chapter 2

## My Dad

I didn't see it coming. One by one, my brothers began to disappear. Every day there was something new to discover, so it was easy to miss the change. But when it was just my sister left, I started to worry. When I whined at Mama, she just looked away. When I barked at Joanne, she just patted my head. And then my sister was gone. I searched and paced. It was a new feeling and I didn't like it. I was alone. Where did they all go? Would I go too?

Mama looked dazed and lost. She circled the pen and smelled each corner. She lay down with a "humph." I nestled into the cradle curve of her belly and she licked me all over. As the day ended and darkness took over, I moved closer and closed my eyes. It would be my last snuggle with Mama.

I woke up to the sounds of Joanne. Mama was gone. Joanne was moving quickly. I had become very familiar with her mornings. They usually started slow and grew into wonderful smells and would eventually bring Joanne to our puppy pen. But this morning was different. Something new was in the air. Joanne buzzed about, slamming doors and talking to herself. Suddenly it got quiet, and Joanne stood at the puppy pen looking down at me.

"OK, pumpkin, it's time. It's your turn."

Her voice was heavy. I looked up at her and whimpered.

"Oh, boo, don't make this harder."

I barked and stood on my back legs.

"You're a lover, little one." Joanne cooed.

My tail flittered. Joanne reached down and picked me up. She rubbed under my chin and then lifted me close to her face. Her lips touched my head.

"Precious, you're gonna do big things."

She squatted, lowered me toward a box, and opened a small door.

"In you go, your very own kennel. It's a present from your new dad."

The box had two windows and a door all made of criss-crossed bars. It was big enough for me to stand and turn around. My blanket was on the floor. It smelled like Mama. My eyes were wide and my heart raced. Joanne picked up my new house, and I was suddenly gliding in the air. My legs were wobbly and my body was thrown against the wall, causing the house to tip to one side. I tried to upright the house by moving to the other side, which only made me slide into the other wall. My stomach started to get queasy so I lay down. We walked into the bright sunshine and down a path until Joanne stood in front of a shiny machine on four wheels. Joanne opened a door and put me inside. The world finally stopped swaying as I landed on something soft. Windows surrounded me. The space smelled like Joanne and other new warm smells. Joanne sat next to me and held a round wheel.

"It's going to be a day of firsts, little one."

Four-wheels rumbled and came to life, and off we rolled.

"TAKE GOOD CARE of him." Joanne sniffled. "Good-bye, sweet boy."

Joanne walked away, leaving me on a long counter. I watched her though the window of my house as she got smaller and smaller in the crowd of humans and then disappeared out a door.

My house lifted off the counter, and we started to move. I looked back at the door where Joanne disappeared. The human carrying my house walked with a bounce that made me lurch forward and back. We moved further and further away from my last sighting of Joanne. I barked at every human we passed, hoping they were Joanne, and then cried when they weren't. Finally I ended up outside the building with a pile of bags I didn't know. The air didn't smell like Joanne's backyard. It was thick with greasy smells. There were rattles and roars, some close and some far away. I shook as I wondered who made those terrible noises. And then I saw her. She was a giant bird with hard-looking wings. All the bags were being thrown onto a moving path. One by one the bags climbed up and then disappeared into the belly of the bird.

"Send up the dog," a voice I couldn't see shouted.

My house lifted with a jolt and landed with a thud on the moving path. I fell against the back wall as my house began to climb up and up. I growled and barked, scratched and cried.

"It's OK, pooch," a human reassured. He was dressed in puffy orange with big pods over his ears. He lifted my house. "Here you go, little guy. We saved this spot for you." I heard his footsteps disappear. There was a sliding whoosh and a cracking slam, then complete darkness. Muffled voices outside soon became silent.

I sniffed the air. I was alone. I cried out. Joanne's happy voice didn't answer. Mama didn't come bounding over the boxes. After a long silence, a vibration started to rattle the bird. I shivered. The bird was moving. Its great body creaked and groaned. The pitter-patter in my chest started to pound. The bird was running. There was a loud whirling roar and my insides bubbled. I was pulled to the back of my house by some invisible hand. I whimpered but only the bird's hum replied. My tail tucked and hugged my butt. My legs let go and I collapsed inside the cold-hearted bird, too scared to close my eyes, too tired to stand. The blanket around me was familiar but provided no comfort. Mama smells were lost in the greasy air and the lifeless bags around me.

At some point in the journey something started to change. It began with a faint tickle in my tummy. My ears felt full. My body began to slowly slide to the front of my house. My tail tapped the floor. The invisible hand continued to push me to the front of my house. Then suddenly the bird took a great jump, several hops, and bellowed a mighty cry. The invisible hand changed direction and yanked me backwards and then let go. We rolled along with a quiet purr and then stopped. I tried to run in circles, but with every turn I slammed into the wall. I came to a fast stop when once again there was a sliding whoosh. Sunlight and human voices welcomed me. I barked.

"Oh my God, you should see this puppy."

A voice further away shouted, "Don't get any ideas. You remember what happened last time you opened a dog door."

I jumped up and banged my head on my roof as I was carried out of the bird.


"EXCUSE ME." A deep voice filled the room. "Is this Alaska cargo?"

My ride in the belly of the bird had only landed me in another lonely room, filled with more bags and boxes and a human dressed in a blue suit.

"Yep, you're in the right place," the blue suit answered.

I let out a high-pitched howl.

The deep voice continued, "I'm here to pick up my dog. Maybe that puppy is mine? My name's Benjamin Walker. He was on a flight from Seattle."

"We've got a boisterous one here," the other voice laughed. "Let me check and see if you win the prize." He shuffled the papers on the counter. "Yup, you're the lucky one." He bent down and peered into my house. "He's gorgeous. How old?"

"A little over eight weeks. I've only seen pictures," the deep voice replied.

"Well, little one, meet your daddy." My house floated up to the counter and I saw the deep-voiced human. He stared into my house with a round face, thick black hair, bushy eyebrows, and big brown eyes that sparkled with water.

"It's pretty awesome, isn't it?" the man behind the counter said. "I remember the first time I saw my puppy. It was love at first sight."

"I've never had a dog before. Can we take him out?"

"I can't but he's yours. Go for it."

Fingers fumbled with my door. I heard a snap and my door opened. I leaped out of my house and into my dad's big, furry arms. I licked his salty face. He laughed and held me close as I wiggled. His body was full and soft. He didn't smell like Joanne. The top layer was fresh and sweet, and underneath he smelled like musk. His clothes were full of human food smells. My tail tapped his chest and my nose traveled his neck in search of food.

"Sure looks like love." The human behind the counter was hairless except for short, red whiskers scattered about his face.

I wiggled out of my dad's arms and onto the counter. Immediately I made a puddle.

"Oh shit, I'm so sorry," my dad mumbled and scooped me back up into his arms.

"It's OK." Red-whiskers shrugged his shoulders. "This counter's seen worse. It's all part of puppyhood. It took my girl a couple months to figure out the pee thing, but eventually she got it. I hope you have lots of pee cleaner. It's really important to take the smell out."

"Yeah, I've got a big bottle."

"That's good. Do you have help? Uh, I mean, uh, are you . . . I mean, is it just you?" Red-whiskers' cheeks turned pink.

"Just me," my dad answered.

"Well, there are some great dog parks in the bay area. Do you live in the city?"

"I'm in the lower Haight on Pierce Street."

"Oh, then you're close to Duboce Park. Maybe I'll see you around. My name's Mike, by the way."

"Oh, OK, yeah, uh, nice to meet you." My dad dropped his eyes. "Well, I should get this little guy home. Thanks again."

My dad stuffed me back into my house. I tried to run out but he closed the door as I threw my body against the bars.

Red-whiskers laughed. "Wow, I think the baby's having a tantrum."

My dad peered into my house. "It's OK, little one." And then more softly, he said, "We're going to be OK."


THE ROLLING OF MY dad's four-wheels finally stopped. "We're here. Welcome home, baby boy. You must be going crazy in that crate. Let's get you out in the backyard."

It was getting dark but a yellow glow lit the street. There were shadows of houses lined up in rows. We got out of four-wheels and walked quickly toward a multi-colored house and up some stairs. My dad opened a door and turned on lights, he moved through a long house without putting me down. I barked and whined as we came out the other end of the house and descended down some steps into darkness. My house landed softly.

"Here we are. Let me turn on the yard lights and get you out of that kennel."

Suddenly there was light. My dad's fingers and hairy knuckles moved toward my door. As he fumbled with the latch, a wiggle moved down my backbone and ended with my butt. I was going to make a run for it. The door opened and I darted out in a full gallop and ran zigzag across the soft lawn. It was enclosed by a tall fence but was open to the sky. A breeze had started to cool the air. As the grass bent beneath my paws, smells wrapped their fingers around my nostrils and pulled my head down into the forest of tiny green shoots, knocking me off my legs. I scooted on my belly and rolled on my back through the sweet green rug, wheezing and sneezing as smells tickled my nose. My dad's laughter broke through my dizzy inhales and I jumped to my feet.

"Come here, little guy." He was sitting on the grass, legs crossed and clapping his hands. "Come on."

A lap held no danger of captivity. I ran bow-legged toward my dad, peeing in short, fast spurts then trotting a few more steps, squirting as I waddled.

My dad shook with laughter. "You're such a little boy!"

I took a running dive and landed with a thud against his chest. He fell backwards, and I was suddenly eye-to-eye and nose-to-nose with this new human. I nuzzled his long, thick nose and licked his full, soft lips. He laughed and tried to cover his face.

"Hey, sssssstop." His laughter came in blasts between gulps of air. "Nooooo."

He wanted more. Laughter always means more. I followed my nose down his hairy chest and tried to explore the dank, fleshy smells inside his shirt.

His hands stopped me and held me close enough to smell but too far to taste.

"It's been a long time since anyone has tried to go down there," he laughed.

I tried to wiggle free but he sat up, put me in his big lap, and started to scratch.

"How's that?"

His hand rubbed my middle back. I stared up, my tail quiet with waiting. His hand worked his way back along my spine and rested on my butt. I twitched in anticipation. His fingers began to scratch that place I can never reach, just above my tail. I wagged double-time.

Something moved in the shadows, and I jumped out of my dad's lap in pursuit. It danced across the grass and I pounced. The wind stopped and everything became still. The leaf was lifeless under my paw.

I turned my head at the sound of my dad's voice. "Hi, Anthony." He was talking into a leashless talking-machine. "Yeah, he's here."

"Jeez, Anthony," my dad laughed, "stop screaming, you sound like one of my seventh grade girls. Aren't you at work?"

"I know it's a psych-ward, but aren't you supposed to act saner than the patients?"

My dad laughed. "I hope the color of the uniform isn't the only difference."

"Yes, he's unbelievable. I got all teary at the airport. I heard his little cries and I just melted. It was almost religious. Don't laugh, but I feel like Jesus—you know that picture of Jesus sitting in the forest with the kids and animals?"

"I know. It's a blast from my past. Mrs. Clayton, my Sunday school teacher, gave me that picture. I used to fall asleep looking at it and dream about being one of those kids. I begged my parents for a pet. But look at me, now I'm Jesus with my own puppy." My dad smiled.

"I said don't laugh." My dad chuckled. "I know the Jesus thing is a stretch."

This place smelled different from Joanne's. The dirt wasn't wet and rotting, instead it was more salty and sandy. I ran to the corner of the lawn, where a raised flowerbed hid in the shadows. I took a running leap and skidded to a stop when I felt the pinch. The fragrance invited me closer but my nose was pricked by another sharp bite. As I tried to get away from the pretty-mean flowers, there was another good-bye jab. I tumbled back to the friendly grass and whimpered back to my dad with my tail curved down.

"Yup, that was him," he chuckled. "He just discovered the roses."

His hand caressed my head. Once I recovered I raced to the corners of the yard and back. I ran circles around my dad, hoping he would chase me. He shook his head and laughed.

"Anthony, you've got to meet him. I've never seen a tail wag this fast, like a propeller. He looks like he's going to take off and fly!"

"He's such a cutie. He's got paws and ears that are five sizes too big, and his nose feels like cold, wet kisses. He wiggles sideways when he walks. You've never seen this much joy. People are never this happy. Well, I don't think I have."

My dad stood up and pulled something out of his pocket. He threw it across the yard. I grabbed it on its first bounce. It was an orange-and-blue ball that squeaked! I pranced past my dad in a victory lap but then stopped dead in my tracks. This strange new place suddenly looked familiar. A large tree trunk rose from the ground with knobby arms full of leaves, just like the one I knew in Joanne's yard. Mama always left her smell at the bottom of the tree. I dropped the ball. My nose traveled the tree bark, around once and then again. I wondered why I couldn't find Mama's sharp, fragrant pee. I raced around the fenced yard looking for anything that smelled like Mama. Back and forth, up and down, nose to the ground, I ran and howled.

"What's the matter?" My dad's voice followed me. "Anthony, he's acting really weird."

I flew past my dad, big circles and smaller circles. I hoped that if I ran fast enough, I might find her.

"He's looking for something."

My tongue hung sideways, dripping wet, as I continued to race around.

"Little one, what's wrong? He won't stop, Anthony, what do you think I should do?"

I was dizzy with running and sniffing.

"OK, he's freaking me out. I'm gonna call the breeder. She said I could call."

"Anthony, I gotta go."

"Love you too. Bye."

I whined and barked at my dad.

He paused and then resumed talking in the talking-machine. "Hi, Joanne. It's Ben Walker, from San Francisco."

"Yeah, he made it. He's really beautiful. Thank you."

"Well, he's acting a little strange. He was fine when we first got home, curious and happy, but now he's running around like he's really distressed. Should I do something?"

"Really? You think that's it? Will he get over it?"

"That makes sense. He's probably very confused."

"Do you think that'll help?"

"OK, I'll give it a try. Thanks."

"Bye."

My dad moved carefully towards me and picked me up. He sat down on a chair and cradled me close to his chest.

"Poor baby, do you miss your Mama?" My dad's eyes glistened as he spoke softly.

I squirmed to get free. My dad rubbed all the right places in all the wrong ways. I twisted and turned. His hands held me tight.

"It's going to be OK, you'll see. Shhhhh." He petted me slowly. "There you go." He was warm, and I felt the slow thump of his body. "Yeah, that's a good boy. Shhhhh."

His voice hummed softly. My wiggles began to have less fight, and my breathing slowed with his. My body felt heavy and limp. My eyes twitched and things started to get blurry. I hadn't closed my eyes in a very long time.

I heard a chuckle, followed by a sniffle, and then my dad whispered, "Little boy, you snore like an old man."

# Chapter 3

# Home

I woke up to soft morning light. I looked through the bars in my house and slowly remembered. I let out a sharp bark. The big bed squeaked, and my dad landed on the floor with a thud. The only clothes that covered his thick hairy body were baggy shorts.

"Guess someone is awake." He peered into my house with a sleepy smile. "Hey munchkin, I need a name for you."

I barked louder.

"OK, OK, just a minute. We need to get you outside." He wrapped a robe around himself and his bare feet slid into two flat things. He picked up my house and we walked to the back door, went outside, down the stairs, and into the backyard. Once in the yard, he opened my door and I ran into the damp grass. I remembered the smells from last night, but it looked different without the shadows. I peed.

"Good boy. What a good boy," my dad said cheerfully. "Want some breakfast?"

I did one loop around the yard and then followed my dad up the stairs. At the top I scampered across a floating floor and peeked over the side at the yard below. I was high above the ground. I backed away.

"Looks different in daylight, huh? Come on inside, little man. You must be hungry."

My dad slid open the big glass door. I ran onto a cold tiled floor and sniffed. The room was full of savory memories. My stomach rumbled. A large table with several chairs sat in the middle of the room on a rug the color of nighttime sky. I took off in a frantic hunt. Humans liked to hide food. The underworld of the table was a good place to start looking. I weaved in and out through the maze of wooden legs. The rug had thick loose nubs, a perfect hiding place. After many laps I finally came upon a crisp, sweet crumb buried in a shaggy tuff. It was obvious that this food had been loved. It had the taste of something that didn't normally get left behind. They must have looked high and low for this one. And where there is one, there is always the chance for more. I scooted out from under the table and continued under the long counter that stretched along one wall. Under-counters could be just as rewarding as under-tables, sometimes more. Joanne hid treasures in every corner but not this house. This human was better at hiding things. I would have to look harder . . . My search was interrupted by the sound of rustling paper and a familiar crackle.

"Want some breakfast? Joanne told me you liked this kind." I recognized the ping and bounce in the metal bowl as he poured.

I abandoned my hunt. A gob of drool formed in my mouth. I jumped and danced around my dad's feet. When he put the bowl down I rushed in.

"Slow down! You're going to get sick."

His voice made me eat faster. I remembered all the fights I had with my brothers and sister over food. The only way to protect your food was to eat it. The bowl emptied way too soon. I ran back to my dad's legs and hopped and hoped.

"That's all, greedy! I was warned about you."

I heard a jingle and click in the front of the house.

"What the heck?" My dad sounded annoyed. I tore off down the long hall to investigate. My dad trotted after me, pulling the rope to his robe tighter. As I arrived, the front door was opening. I ran between bare legs perched on tippy-toe shoes.

"Judy, grab him, don't let him down the stairs," my dad shouted.

Soft hands with bright orange nails picked me up, and I ascended to the smell of sweet flowers.

"OOOOO, look at you, ohhhh."

I licked her face. She laughed and shook her head, making her blonde curls bounce. Even with shoes that made her grow, she was much shorter than my dad. Her chest hung big and heavy from a straight and strong back.

"It's awful early. You could have let me know you were coming over or at least rang the doorbell," my dad said sharply.

"Why?"

"It's what people do. I gave you those keys for emergencies."

"I was in the neighborhood and I wanted to meet the baby. Look at him? He is such a sweetie pie. Can you stand it?" Judy's words were juicy and wet.

My dad stood with his arms folded.

"Oh, don't be such a grump. You don't have any secrets from me, no surprises anymore, right?" Judy's long eyelashes danced up and down as she talked.

"That's not the point."

Judy put me down on the floor and rubbed my head. "He really is one of the most gorgeous puppies I've ever seen."

I rolled over on my back with my feet in the air.

Judy laughed and rubbed my belly. "Shameless . . . good for you! Get all you can, for as long as you can. You never know when the well runs dry. Does he have a name yet?"

"No."

"What does he think of his new home?"

"He hasn't had a chance to check it out yet. We got home last night and he was exhausted. He basically passed out, so we just went to bed. We were just about to explore when you barged in."

"I can leave." Judy moved toward the front door.

My dad sighed. "Forget it, you're already here."

"I thought so." Judy tossed her hair and spun around. "Come on pint-size, let's check out your new home." She started down the hallway, "Ben, why are all the doors closed?"

"He needs a chaperone wherever he goes. He's a puppy." Judy reached for a doorknob. My dad lunged for the door and held it closed. "No, it's a total mess in there. I started an oil painting last week, my paints are everywhere."

"Fine, but you know he's going to get in there someday. You won't be able to hide anything from him." She looked at my dad and raised her eyebrows.

"Very funny." My dad sighed.

I hippity-hopped around their feet, trying to get noticed.

Judy continued, "Has Anthony been here yet? I wanted to meet the puppy before him."

"He's coming over this afternoon. You know, it's not a competition. It's hard to believe you used to be friends."

"Things change." Judy shrugged her shoulders.

I barked.

Judy bent down and patted my head. "Come on, love, let's go bust down some doors." Judy led us down the hallway and opened the next door. "I guess you've already seen the bedroom, sweet-ums."

I ran in.

Judy stood in the doorway. "Where does he sleep?"

I crawled under my dad's bed, expecting to find something interesting, but I didn't even find dust puffs. The ones at Joanne's used to make me sneeze.

My dad pointed at my house. "He's going to sleep in his kennel until he's house broken. That's what all the books say."

"And I'm sure you've read all the books. Come on, pipsqueak, keep up with the tour." Judy returned to the hall and opened the next door. I raced past her. "Here's the bathroom. Your dad spends lots of time in here."

My dad shook his head. "Yeah, right. No one spends more time in a bathroom than you."

Judy fluffed her hair. "That's because I'm the pretty one."

My dad smiled. "You got me there."

The room was wet with sweet smells that hid previous funk. A long white tail hung from the wall. I grabbed the end with my teeth and started to run. The tail grew longer and longer.

Judy laughed. "Puppies always go for the toilet paper."

My dad was suddenly in the water-room. "Hey, stop, leave it." He picked me up and tried to take away the soft tail. I shook my head and the tail melted in my mouth.

"He's no fun, is he?" Judy opened another door.

I wiggled out of my dad's arms and ran full speed into the new room with lots of places for humans to sit. My paws slid on the shiny and slippery floor as I rammed into a wall and tumbled head over tail. My dad and Judy laughed. I felt a rush of wildness as I jumped up and ran as fast as I could, darting in and out of the furniture, nails scratching and sliding around every corner. Suddenly a low table appeared out of nowhere. There was no way to avoid it and I crashed into it. The table wobbled slowly, followed by a clattering smash of water, flowers, and little sharp chunks.


MY DAD HELD ME in his arms as he and Judy stood at the front door. "Next time, a little heads-up, please?"

Judy crossed her arms. "Fine."

My dad looked softer. "I can't believe he broke the Waterford."

Judy patted my head. "I've a feeling this isn't going to be the last act of destruction — no more house-beautiful. It's just a thing."

"No, it's not. It was my favorite wedding present. We got it from your mom."

Judy smiled sadly.

My dad continued, "I loved that vase."

Judy kissed my dad's cheek. "It's all about letting go . . . didn't you tell me that once?" She paused. "Well, I should be going."

My dad held me up near Judy's face. "Say good-bye to your auntie. Tell her thanks for visiting and next time to call."

"And you tell your dad to relax." Judy kissed my head. "Bye, sweetness." She then looked over at my dad. "Not you."

"Bye, Judy." My dad rolled his eyes and closed the door.

MY DAD MOVED about the eating-room. A piercing shrill noise came from the counter in a long and then a short burst. A familiar smell floated in the room. Joanne used to make the same dark, burnt smell in the mornings. Before long there was a gurgling and bubbling sound that increased the scent. Unexpectedly, a bell rang from the front of the house. I knew that good things usually happened when bells rang. I raced to the front door.

My dad followed. "What the heck? What'd she forget," he grumbled and picked me up. He scrunched his face against the door, as if looking through it, and then laughed. "Get ready, little one, you're about to meet Anthony." He opened the door.

"Good morning, PAPA," a loud voice teased.

"OHHH." The loud voice looked at me and hushed to a whisper. "Look at him. I'm gonna cry." He flapped his arms like wings.

"Jeez, Anthony! I thought you were going to take a nap before you came over?"

The human standing at the door was a mix of things that didn't go together. He was big like my dad but looked stronger. His thick neck and broad shoulders looked scary, but when he moved and spoke he looked more like a dancing dog with bows. His light-green uniform hung tightly to his body, revealing his many bulges. He had shiny black hair and smooth, tan skin.

"There was no way I could sleep knowing this guy was here."

I tried to get out of my dad's arms.

"Would you look at all that LOVE? Ben, he's gorgeous!" Anthony's mouth shined with big white teeth.

"Well, get in the house so I can put him down without him running out the door."

Anthony floated in.

"Come here, precious one. Give your uncle some love." Anthony lowered his bulk to the floor and kneeled.

I ran over to him and bounced up and down. He wrestled me to the ground and pinned me with his gigantic hand. Then he scampered away on his hands and knees as I chased. Suddenly he stopped, made happy growls, and then took off after me.

Finally, he collapsed and spread out on the floor. I climbed up the firm flesh mountain and crawled straight for his face.

"Hey, not on the lips . . . stop it . . . it's only our first date."

We rolled around the floor. Anthony gulped air in between screams and laughter. He played like a big puppy. I got more and more excited. My teeth found the fleshy part of his arm.

"OUCH!" Anthony yelled. I froze and crouched low to his chest. "Easy there, little boy, slow down." Anthony began to scratch my ears. He sat up and looked at my dad. "He gets a little carried away, doesn't he?"

My dad pulled up his sleeves and pointed to his arms. "He thinks that love should leave teeth marks."

"He's perfect." Anthony stood up, leaving me on the floor. He wrapped his arms around my dad and lifted him off the ground. "He's gonna be good for you."

"Put me down, you'll get a hernia," my dad groaned.

I ran around Anthony's feet and barked.

Anthony set my dad down. "*Someone* doesn't like to be ignored."

"Yeah, he's not shy about asking for what he wants."

"There's a lesson for you." Anthony winked at my dad.

"Yeah, right . . . come on, I haven't had my coffee yet and I've got sticky buns from Tartine." My dad started to walk down the hallway.

I suddenly remembered I was full, overflowing actually. I squatted.

Anthony pointed and shouted, "BEN, he's peeing!"

My dad spun around and charged toward me. "NO." I tightened and the pee stopped. He scooped me up in his arms and sprinted toward the back door with Anthony running behind, laughing.

Outside I finished what I started.

"Atta boy, good boy." My dad handed me a chewy treat. "Come on, Anthony, give the kid some kudos."

Anthony was still chuckling. "You boys put on quite the show. Way to go . . . what'd you name him?'

"I haven't yet. Any suggestions?"

"How about Reese? With all that chocolate and tan he looks like a Reese's Peanut Butter Cup." Anthony picked me up and rubbed his nose against mine. "And I could just eat you up."

"Hang around a bit and you might reconsider. You wouldn't believe what he puts in his mouth. If it's nasty and disgusting, he's all over it. But let's not go there, I need some coffee."

We followed my dad back into the house. My dad moved quickly in the eating-room, opening doors and drawers. Every clang and bang brought hopes of a second breakfast. When my dad sat down at the eating-room table with two steaming cups, I ran to my bowl to check.

"So, any good gossip?" my dad said as he took a sip.

"Well, I met this really cute bear at the Eagle beer bust on Sunday."

"You and furry things."

"Big furry things." Anthony grinned.

My bowl was empty. I ran over to the fleshy legs that dangled under the table. There was no clear way up, so I jumped and cried.

My dad lifted me into his lap and petted my head. "Anthony, do you know how many Abercrombie hearts you've broken? They think the smooth and muscled tribe should all stay together."

"Where's the fun in that? Love is all about getting what you don't have."

I wanted more than a rub. I reached for the table and tried to climb up. "Oh, no you don't!" My dad pulled me back. "No table privileges for you." He put me on the floor. "I don't think that's called love; I think it's called lust. I'm not judging, mind you, it's great someone's getting some."

"Don't sound so pathetic. You and this adorable dog could stop traffic."

I whined.

My dad picked me up. "I hate the gym. I love to eat. I hate the bars. I love being home. I think I'm getting old."

"You're only thirty-four."

"Maybe I'd just rather date vicariously. You can keep me entertained with your stories."

Anthony shook his head. "Such a waste!"

I tried once more to pull myself up to the table so I could see. "No," my dad said more sternly, "not the table." He put me back on the floor.

I yelped. This time my dad reached down and patted my head. I barked and clawed on my dad's leg.

"Wow, this little guy is needy," Anthony chuckled. "Come over here, little one, Uncle will take care of you." His fingers snapped under the table, and I ran to the invitation. He picked me up and scooted away from the table and held me in his lap, petting me with his heavy hands. "He really does have beautiful hair. It's so soft and silky."

"I know. You know what's weird? I had this memory this morning when I was petting him — my mom's hair was the same color, same texture. Isn't that strange?"

Anthony's eyes twinkled. "You mean in a neurotic, Freudian wish-fulfillment kind of way?"

"Screw you. Save your psychobabble for your patients."

"Ben, your dog has beautiful hair, period. How about you leave your mom out of this relationship? He's a dog."

"I know. It's depressing that she still pops up in my head after all these years. It's like we have an umbilical cord that can't ever be cut. Sometimes I think that emancipation isn't possible in my family."

"Wow, don't go dark on me. We're celebrating this puppy, remember?"

My dad continued. "I wonder what it's like for a dog? I mean, this little guy will probably never see his mom again. Last night he carried on like a maniac. I think he was trying to find her."

Anthony rubbed my ears. "Yes, and look at him now, all content and happy. He's a testament to resilience and moving on."

They continued talking, but the weight and warmth of Anthony's hand made my eyes droopy. Their voices drifted away.

I woke up to the sound of moving chairs.

"I should get going and let you get out of your bath robe." Anthony stood up. "Why don't you come out with me tonight? I'm going to the Powerhouse. Celebrate summer vacation. It'll be fun."

"It's not my scene. Besides, I now have a child." My dad took me out of Anthony's arms. "I should get him out to the backyard. They say the best way to train him to pee outside is to limit the chances that he could have an accident."

Anthony shook his head.

"Maybe next time." My dad shrugged his shoulders.

"Ben, I really do worry about you. It feels like you're trying to disappear."

"That's not true. You always know where you can find me."

Anthony sighed. "Yeah, but you're always alone."

My dad hugged me. "Not anymore."

Anthony came over and wrapped his arms around us. I was smashed in between their sweat. They smelled pungent and different.

"I love you, Ben," Anthony said softly.

"Me too," my dad replied.


THE DAY HAD been full of new things but, as with all days, eventually it grew dark and quiet. My house seemed way too small. I barked and scratched at the door.

"It's time for bed, wild child," my dad said from his bed.

I was just getting used to life without bars. I whined.

"Go to sleep, little guy . . . please."

I tried to dig through the floor of my house, but my blanket bunched under my nose. Mama's scent in my blanket filled my nostrils, the dark musky smell of her hair. I remembered her funky, stale breath. I started to moan. My dad was very quiet. I threw myself against my door and cried.

"Listen, kid, we've got to sleep."

I heard the floor creak and soft footsteps. My dad dropped his blankets on the floor. He got down on his hands and knees and then lay down next to my house.

"Shhhh."

I could smell him.

"It's OK. It's you and me now. Shhhh. That's a good puppy."

His voice was husky and low. His fingers appeared through the bars of my door. I licked their warm sweetness.

"That's right, it's your daddy. Shhhh."

His fingers scratched my neck as his smell mixed with Mama's. I curled up against my door and sighed good-bye to Mama and goodnight to my dad.

# Chapter 4

## Leave It

I woke up shaking with excitement. All the changes were behind me, like a fading whiff of runny poo. I sniffed the air. Smells, who knew where they could lead? All I had to do was inhale and follow my nose. Anything was possible—maybe something completely new, so fantastic that all the other discoveries would seem like day-old water, slimy and stale.

My dad slid his legs off his bed. His hair was wild and twisted. He stood and stretched toward the ceiling. His round belly tightened, and a tent protruded from his shorts. I barked from behind my bars. He started to lower his arms and then stopped mid-air. He closed his eyes.

"Shit," he mumbled and hurried out of the room.

I heard the water-room door open and slam, followed by a groan, gurgles and blops, silence, and then a rush of water. I circled my house, tempted to relieve the pressure that was building.

But the house rules, rules I knew but had never been taught, said "don't do it." So I held it and whined. Finally my dad returned to the sleeping-room draped in his fluffy robe. He peered down at my house.

"Good morning, little guy." His voice was slow and friendly, but his face was creased with lines of worry. "So, what kind of day do you think we're going to have today? Mine hasn't started so great."

He looked troubled, possibility muzzled by too many nos. My dad opened my door and I danced out.

"Just a minute, mister. First, you've got to take care of some business outside. After you pee, we can have breakfast and go for a real walk."

He picked me up and my wiggles paused. My nose found his mouth. His breath smelled like soured food.

My dad blew into my face. "That's morning breath. I know it's funky, but you probably like that."


"WOW, WHAT A beautiful day. Want to check out the neighborhood?" My dad stood in the open door as sunshine beamed in. "We better enjoy it because June gloom will be back before we know it."

I chewed on the "no" that he had just snapped on to my collar.

"Hey, leave that alone." My dad gave the leash a quick tug. "Come on, let's go."

We headed down the stairs, but the leash pulled this way and that, usually where I didn't want to go. It wrapped around my legs, and I tumbled down the last three stairs.

"Are you hurt?" My dad bent down and ran his hand over me like something was wrong. "You're supposed to take those one at a time." He sounded worried and mad at the same time. "You better slow down. You're going to get hurt."

I gave my body a quick shake and took off. There were bushes on the side of the stairs. I moved quickly to investigate. They were filled with a medley of pee smells, but the freshest one was still wet.

"Get out of there, that looks like dog piss." My dad's voice was sharp. He pulled the leash.

I'd seen a glimpse of what was before me on the night I had arrived, but this place was unlike anything I had ever seen. There were lots of hard surfaces with lonely trees, a few plants here and there, and even less grass. Houses of many colors lined each side, touching each other, one after another. Some four-wheels were parked, others whizzed by, some honked, others hummed. I darted from one green thing to the next, criss-crossing in front and then behind my dad.

"You're crazy. Can't you pick a side and stay there?" My dad shook his head and chuckled.

I stopped in my tracks, nose to the cement. A tangy, gooey blob was smeared into the sidewalk."

"Stop . . . leave it," he said sternly.

It was clear my dad couldn't smell the possibility. I pulled it free and swallowed it whole.

"Great. I wonder how long it takes to poop out bubble gum."

I set off to look for more. The sidewalk held amazing discarded treats. Some were only leftover paper wrappings, but others lay boldly waiting to be devoured. My dad tried to keep me from every find.

"Leave it," his worried voice followed as I sniffed.

If my dad saw it, it was his, but if I got there first and ate it, it was mine! I darted over to a young tree growing out of a hole in the sidewalk. A pile of black poo lay at the base, faint hints of its fragrant past crusted over with time.

"Gross, stop, get away from that." There was another yank from the leash.

"Oh . . . Mrs. Harris, hi, how are you today?" My dad's voice abruptly turned sweet.

I looked up. Ahead of us a human was bending over pots filled with lush green plants. Her hair was white and wooly and her skin was dark brown.

Her voice rose slow and strong. "I'm blessed. And you?"

"I'm doing OK. Your flowers look great."

"Thank you. The roses are doing well this year." Her head tilted sidewise and her eyes settled on me. "And who do we have here?"

Her friendly voice called me. I strained to get closer.

"This is my new puppy. I just got him two days ago. It's our first walk and he's getting into everything. Everything he shouldn't, that is. I feel like all I do is say *no*."

"That's what he's supposed to do. He's a baby figuring out the world." She removed a glove and held out her hand. "Come here, love."

She moved toward us slowly. When she was close enough, my dad let out just enough leash for my nose to touch her hand. I smelled food. I wiggled as I licked fruity sweetness from her bony fingers.

My dad kept the leash taut. "I just don't want him to get sick. He hasn't had all his shots, and he has no sense of what's good for him."

Mrs. Harris smiled. "You sound like a parent." She petted my head.

My dad let me inch closer. "I haven't seen your son around in a while."

"James is so busy with work and his family. You know, he got a promotion at his law firm. He's working so hard. His youngest is walking now. She's a handful. The oldest is eight and playing soccer."

"When's the last time you saw them?"

"February, for my birthday," she said sadly.

"That's four months ago. That's a long time. Sacramento isn't that far. I hope they spend some of their summer vacation with you."

"We'll see."

"You know you can call me if you need anything? School's over so I'm on summer vacation. With the puppy, I don't plan on going anywhere."

"Thank you, that's very sweet, but I'm getting on fine. You know I have my church family. How are *you* feeling?"

"Pardon?"

"Last time I saw you, you said your stomach was bothering you and that you had to hurry home. I think the flu is going around."

"Oh . . . that . . . I'm better, thank you."

"Well, I've been praying for you."

"Thank you, Mrs. Harris. Well, we should finish our walk." My dad gave my leash a tug.

"Do you have time for some cobbler?" Mrs. Harris asked. "I just made it."

"That sounds great, but I really need to give the puppy a walk."

"How about after your walk? Oh, and bring this little guy, I think I've got some dog treats around." Mrs. Harris rubbed my back.

"Are you sure? He's a little wild."

"Oh, he's just excited. We all could take a lesson from him," Mrs. Harris smiled.

MRS. HARRIS'S house was warm and stuffy. The walls had no empty spaces and all the surfaces were piled high with stuff. There were old smells and everything looked well used, except the front room where all the sitting places were zipped in a slippery, clear wrapping. I dashed about, tongue dripping from my mouth.

My dad's voice followed me. "No, not that, leave it."

Mrs. Harris watched us. "Oh, don't fuss about him. There's nothing in here that's so precious that it can't handle a puppy sniff."

"It's not the smelling I'm worried about. He's a chewer."

"Oh, he's a toddler, isn't he?" Mrs. Harris chuckled. "Look at him! Everything's a new adventure. Let's go to the kitchen. I've got something for him."

Once in the eating-room, Mrs. Harris found a bag. "Here, dear." She lowered her hand and opened her fist. A smoky scent wafted to my nose. "This should keep him busy for a while. Ben, would you mind making some coffee? The coffee is in that Tupperware box on the counter."

"Sure." My dad started moving things around on the eating-room counter.

I chewed but watched my dad in case anything else dropped to the floor.

"Wow, your cobbler looks wonderful," my dad said, as the sound of water filled a pot.

"Thank you. I canned the peaches last summer and I thought I better use them up before peach season starts. Could you dish it up?"

I jumped up and whimpered.

"Someone wants another snack," Mrs. Harris said with a sparkle.

"No begging. Finish what you've got," my dad said as he put dishes on the table.

"He's not begging, just hoping. There's a difference. Right, little puppy?"

"If you say so," my dad smiled. He scooped out something and put it onto two plates. A brown nugget tumbled over the side of the table. I ran over and claimed it.

"That's what I love about dogs," Mrs. Harris chuckled. "They are always ready to seize an opportunity."

"I never thought about it that way." My dad paused, "You're always so positive."

Mrs. Harris sighed, "Hmmm, I just try to see the blessing."

My dad looked on the wall above the table. "I didn't know you had two sons. Are they twins?"

"Yes, they were identical twins but different in every way."

"Where does your other son live?"

Mrs. Harris took a bigger sigh. "Oh, he's passed on. We lost him in 1982."

My dad's face softened. "I'm so sorry."

Mrs. Harris's eyes glistened. "There's not a day that goes by that I don't think about Rob."

My dad shifted in his seat. "He was so young, was it unexpected?"

Mrs. Harris was quiet for a moment. "We drifted apart. He used to tell me everything, but at some point I didn't like what he was telling me so he stopped talking to me. He thought I was angry, but it wasn't anger. I was scared. Mothers are supposed to protect their children, and I didn't know how to protect Rob."

"What did you need to protect him from?"

"Society, bigotry, hatred, himself . . . I didn't understand him, but I knew he could get hurt. And yet I participated in a code of silence. My church doesn't like to talk about some things. Rob died of AIDS."

"I'm sorry. Must have been hard for your other son, being a twin and all."

"I think it's why he doesn't like to come around much. I suppose he blames me. It's a terrible thing to lose a child."

"I can't imagine." My dad paused. "I have the opposite problem. My mother died when I was twelve."

"Oh, I'm sorry. I think I knew. A mother can sense a motherless child."

"It's a long time ago. She had lots of problems."

"Well then, I think God put you in my heart for a reason."

The room got silent.

My dad ate something from his plate. "The cobbler is delicious."

"Glad you like it." Mrs. Harris reached into the treat bag. "And don't worry, I won't forget *you*, my dear." She held out her hand and gave me another chew.

# Chapter 5

## Let's Play

When you start to get to know a new place, every detail is important. Everything is a hint about what is yet to come. At the end of each day, when the sunlight was long gone, my dad would open the door to my house, point, and say, "Go to your bed." There was always a treat that followed me, so I was happy to go in.

Exploring my new world was exhausting. As I scooted into my house, I loved the way the blankets nested in between those walls that held me tight, just right. Sleep comes easy when roaming is not an option. But as light made its first peek, as it always did, and turned night into day, those walls closed in. Just right became all-wrong. I was a captive, unable to start my day until my dad set me free.

Strange, how a house can be a home and a cage. Some mornings he rose with the birds with a friendly and happy voice, and other mornings he moved dazed and slow with grunts and growls. The hint was often buried in the night. Sometimes he had a peaceful quiet sleep and sometimes had a restless sleep with whimpering dreams.

I WAS DIZZY with thoughts of pee and my legs twitched for the open hallway. I watched his bed for clues. All I could see from my house on the floor was the mound of him wrapped in blankets. It moved up and down in a slow and steady dance with his gravelly breaths. Sunshine peeked through the hanging-window-blankets in long blades of light. All of my whines and cries went unnoticed.

*Ring. Ring.*

My dad's arms fumbled to find their way out of the soft cave that hid all but his face.

"Hello," he said slow and hoarse.

"What?"

"Who?"

"What time is it?"

"Give me a break, Harvey, it's summer vacation."

"I had a shitty night."

"No, I didn't have a late night. I was in bed by ten."

"It's called the San Francisco Pride Parade and no I didn't go."

"I'm not taking a tone with you. I just woke up."

"I don't know why; I just couldn't sleep. It happens sometimes. What do you want?"

"Well, you don't usually call to just say hi."

"Good idea, call me later."

"Bye."

My dad put the talking-machine down hard. I barked.

"Shut up." He rolled over and stared at me. After a long silence he mumbled, "That's the way it is, my dad bites me and then I bite you. Don't you love being part of this family?"

There was another ring. My dad growled and grabbed the talking-machine.

"What?"

"Oh," his tone changed, "hey Anthony, I thought you were my dad."

"No, it's OK. I just don't want to talk to *him*. It's amazing how quickly he can piss me off."

"I didn't do anything. I had a horrible night and he wanted to interrogate me."

"He's not concerned. When he sees weakness, he just likes to stir the pot."

"No, I haven't told him. It never seems like the right time. Maybe he knows or suspects, but I come from a family with a long tradition of putting our heads in the sand."

"Maybe . . . some day."

"I don't know why he called. There must have been something in the news about the gay parade because he wanted to know if I went. I basically hung up on him."

"I know I'm a shit but I have good reasons."

"He resented me and I was just a kid. They never should have married, and she didn't believe in divorce. Harvey resented my relationship with my mom and she certainly didn't help that dynamic."

"I could just tell. He never said anything. He just acted like he wished I wasn't there."

"No, it wasn't all bad. There was that time we went camping after Mom died. I was a teenager and didn't want to go. I couldn't imagine spending a week with him. I suppose he wasn't thrilled, either. But something lifted when we were alone and in nature. I don't remember talking much, but we did lots of fishing. There was something good about being in that boat doing our own thing but the same thing. Do you remember those stages of development in child development class? I think it's called parallel play—two kids sharing a sandbox without the expectation of cooperation. The sad thing is that Harvey and I never advanced to the next stage. Mom and then her death took up too much room in the sandbox."

I started to whine and scratch my house.

"The natives are getting restless. I should get him outside and get this day started."

"I'll try. Is it foggy outside?"

"That's good. Maybe there's hope the sun will win today."

"I can't help it. I've got seasonal affective disorder."

"I do. I'm sure of it. That's why you're good for me."

My dad smiled. "Talk to you later, sunshine."


MY DAD WAS restless. I followed him from room to room. He shuffled stuff from place to place, taking the things that were out and putting them behind doors and inside drawers. I like my stuff out where I can see it.

The sitting-room had a basket with crumpled, soft white things filled with little salty treats. To my amazement and delight, they grew wings when I shredded and tossed them in the air.

"Gross. Not the Kleenexes," he yelled as he stomped toward me.

My dad took all of my fluttering friends, put them back in the basket, and then placed them out of reach. I followed him into the sleeping-room where he began to rearrange the blankets on his bed. An animal-skin-with-strings lay under the bed. The outside tasted gamey and wild and the inside tasted like my dad's feet.

There was another shout. "NO! Leave it, those are my good shoes."

I tore off with the prize hanging from my mouth. My dad ran after me and then stole it. It seemed every find turned into a no.

As the day moved on and started to lose its light, my dad finally gave up his wandering and sat down in the sitting-room. Of all the rooms in my dad's house, the sitting-room was the least fun. It usually was just a matter of time before the sitting-room became the sitting-looking-room. He just couldn't ignore his looking-boxes. My dad held something in his hands and every so often he pointed it at the looking-box that talked and flashed colors. Every push made the noise change. He looked long and hard and I felt him floating further and further away. I thought I was going to disappear. I let out a howl that made him see me.

"Shhh, take a nap. Let me watch some TV."

His hand dropped off the chair and landed with a half-hearted rub.

"There's nothing on," he sighed.

He got up and moved over to the other looking-box. It was even more selfish. It demanded both his hands. His fingers tapped its lap and it responded with clicks. I sat and stared, trying to get my dad to look down.

"You've got mail." I cocked my head. It could talk too.

My dad's fingers moved quickly. "No way," he mumbled and then added, "I'm not that desperate." His fingers continued to tap and once in awhile one of his hands moved and caressed its tail.

"Thanks, but not a match," he said in a slow voice as his fingers moved up and down.

"Hmmmm . . . Yeah, right, like I even have a chance." More clicking, looking, and caressing.

"You've got mail," the box said again.

"Wow, he's hot," my dad said in that same slow voice as his fingers tapped.

He sat and stared at the box. He waited and waited and waited. Nothing happened.

"Flake," my dad finally said with irritation and started making the box click again.

"You've got mail."

My dad smiled. "Look at that, he's still interested . . . just an AOL crash." His fingers started up again.

"You've got mail."

He reached down and patted my head. "He wants to know what I'm up to. I wonder if he likes dogs."

"You've got mail."

My dad laughed. "He says he's a cute pup with tricks and he want's to come over. What should I tell him?"

"You've got mail."

My dad took a deep breath. "He *really* wants to come over. What the heck?"

My dad tapped his fingers and the box beeped, moaned, and then went blank. He looked down at me. "His name is Thomas and he's on his way. You better give your old man a break tonight. Don't steal the show!" My dad had a hint of fun in his voice that I hadn't heard all day. He reached down and grabbed my nose. I shook my head and nipped at his fingers.

He laughed but stood up and left the sitting-room and headed down the hallway to the water-room. I followed, expecting that we would play. Once in the water-room he took off his clothes. He stood in front of the looking-back-window.

He shrugged his shoulders. "His profile said he likes husky."

He opened the sliding see-through door, stepped into the big white trough, and slid the door closed. I stood up on my hind legs and saw my dad as water fell down on him. Sweet smells wafted over the door.

"All I want to do . . . is make sweet love to you," my dad sang and swayed.

The water-room began to get warmer and filled up with water smoke. I could tell that something exciting was about to happen.


WHEN THE doorbell rang, I ran to the front door but my dad walked to the water- room. Confused, I ran back. My dad sprayed his neck with something that smelled like spicy wet leaves. It made me sneeze as it floated to the floor. Then he turned with his back to the looking-back-window and stretched his neck around so he could see. He turned around again and faced the looking-back-window.

"Wish me luck, little one," he smiled.

I've never understood looking-back-windows. My dad spent a lot of time in front of it. As far as I could tell he always saw the same thing. And yet sometimes he'd smile like he'd just met an exciting new friend. And sometimes he'd wrinkle his face and shake his head like he'd just seen someone he didn't like.

My dad picked me up in his arms and walked toward the door. I was very excited. I could feel my dad's heart thumping against my belly. I licked his fingers.

"Slow down, fella, we don't want to appear too eager."

All of a sudden my dad stopped. "Shit." He walked quickly back to the eating- room. He picked up several small plastic bottles on the counter. He opened a cupboard door, and they rattled as he hid them inside.

The doorbell rang again. He quickly walked back to the front door and opened it. A young man stood there, smiling. He had small dark eyes and thin, tight pink lips. His hair was thick and black. One of his pant legs was rolled up to his shin. A two-wheel leaned against him.

"Hey, I'm Thomas."

"Hi, I'm Ben, and this is . . . I haven't named him yet," my dad said as he rubbed my head.

"He's really cute," Thomas said while looking at my dad.

"Yeah, and unfortunately he knows it," my dad laughed. "Come on in. You can leave your bike in the hallway."

Once Thomas was in the house, my dad put me on the floor. I danced and hopped around Thomas's feet.

"He likes you," my dad smiled.

"I love dogs but they're a lot of responsibility. I'm more of a cat person. They pretty much take care of themselves," Thomas replied and then added, "But your dog is a sweetheart."

"Well, come on in. I'll get us something to drink."

They walked toward the back of the house, and I ran circles around their feet.

"Nice place," Thomas said as he stopped in front of the doorway to the sleeping-room. "Do you live alone?"

"Yep, just me . . . and now the pup, how about you?"

"I have two roommates, two straight guys," Thomas replied. "I just graduated from Berkeley. We were in a fraternity together."

"How does that work?"

"They're pretty cool. But they don't know that I fool around with guys so I don't play at home." Thomas paused and then added, "I'm bisexual."

"Oh, OK, I guess that's cool."

When they got to the eating-room my dad asked, "Would you like some water?"

"Do you have anything with a little more punch?" Thomas grinned.

"No, sorry, I don't drink, but I think I've got some juice."

"How about some Mary Jane?" Thomas winked.

"Sorry, I don't smoke, either. Guess I'm kinda boring."

"Hey, no problem, it's not like I need anything. Just thought it would be fun. Some water would be great," Thomas said quickly.

My dad began to fill two glasses with water.

Thomas moved in close behind him and wrapped his arms around my dad's waist. "This doesn't look boring. You look even hotter in person." He put his face next to my dad's neck and inhaled. "Patchouli drives me crazy."

My dad made a gravelly groan and turned around. "Mmm, you move fast."

"Only when I see something I like." Thomas opened his mouth like he was eating my dad's neck and then moved down toward my dad's chest. His voice was smooth. "I especially like this view." Thomas pulled my dad's shirt open. "I love your hairy chest." He pressed his body into my dad.

Something was going to happen. I ran to the front of the house to get my orange-and-blue ball. When I got back my dad's and Thomas's lips were stuck together. Their bodies were pushing against each other and the groans grew louder. I dropped my ball by their feet and waited for someone to pick it up and throw it. Neither of them even looked down. They began to pet each other, hands moving everywhere.

I started to whine and run around the eating-room. Thomas moved his hands down to my dad's pants. I heard a snap and zip. Next thing I knew my dad's pants dropped to the floor and fell into a pile around his ankles. I ran over and took a bite of his pants and started to pull.

"Whoa, wait, just wait, just a minute." My dad bent down and pushed me away. He pulled his pants up.

"What's the matter? Is it the dog?" Thomas asked. Before my dad could answer, Thomas added, "We could go to your bedroom."

There was a long silence and then my dad said, "No, that's not it. It's just a little too fast."

My dad snapped his pants.

Thomas cocked his head. "I don't get it. You seemed into it?"

"I was . . . I am . . . it's not you . . . I'm sorry, I just can't."

"We have a hot conversation online, you invite me over, make out with me, and then you just can't?"

"It's me . . . I'm sorry."

"Well, OK." Thomas rolled his eyes and shook his head. "Should I go?"

"We could hang out for awhile and talk." My dad looked at the floor.

"No, I think I should go." Thomas turned toward the hallway.

"I'm really sorry." My dad followed Thomas to the front door. "Thanks for coming over."

Thomas took his two-wheels and walked out the door. My dad stared at the closed door and turned the lock. I barked and stood on my back paws. He bent down and picked me up. Water started to run down his cheeks. Something deep inside me stirred. I wanted to make the water stop.

"What's the point?" my dad sighed. "Why do I even try?"

I licked the warm water from his face.

# Chapter 6

# Beau

Humans love their words. Words are like a wag before a butt sniff or a growl before a bite. Words tell you that something is about to happen, sometimes, but not always. The confusing thing about words is that they're not all the same. Some are important, and others just buzz around like flies on a warm summer day. Who can tell the difference?

My dad held my head in his hands and stared at me. "I've got to decide on a name or you'll have issues. How about *Beau*? I think I'm going to call you *Beau*."

The damp wind whipped around the backyard. My dad was wrapped in extra layers. A gray sky lay heavy on top of us.

"Brrrr! How about it, Beau? Should we go look for some real summer today?"

The air was damp and wild. It teased my nose with new smells and then ran away before I could get a good whiff. I ducked out of my dad's hold. The cool made me bounce.

"If only we could go to the East Bay, they'd probably have sun. We're almost done with your shots. Soon you'll be able to play with the big boys. Can't wait to take you on the Joaquin Miller trail."

My dad held out his hand.

"Come. Come here, Beau."

I ran to the open palm and gobbled up the treat.

"Beau, that's a good boy. Hmmm . . . Beau . . . I like it."

"THANKS FOR coming over." My dad sat across from Judy in the sitting-room. "Don't you hate this weather?"

"It's why Mark Twain said the coldest winter he ever spent was a summer in San Francisco. Don't be such a wimp."

My dad watched Judy and then crossed his arms.

Judy picked me up and held me in her lap. She petted me without looking at my dad. The room was silent except for my breathing that became heavier with every stroke.

My dad's voice eventually interrupted the quiet. "You know I hate when there's tension."

"Well then, stop being tense." Judy rolled me over and rubbed my belly.

My dad shifted in his seat. "You aren't going to make this easy, are you?"

"What are you talking about?"

"Fine. I'm sorry I hurt your feelings the other day."

Judy finally looked at my dad.

He continued, "You can't just barge into my house anytime you want."

"Duh!"

My dad looked out the window and the room was again filled with quiet. I moved so Judy could rub my other side. Her hand roamed easy across all my soft spots, stopping to gently scratch the parts that didn't know they needed scratching until she found them. The room began to dim as my eyes began to get heavy.

"Guess what?" My dad suddenly sounded bright. "I think I have a name for the puppy. I think you'll like it."

"Oh?" Judy replied.

"The other day I was depressed about something, and I swear the little guy tried to cheer me up. It's like he could sense something was wrong, and he wanted to do something about it."

"He's special," Judy said as her hand rubbed under my chin.

My dad paused. "Well, he reminded me of Claire. Your mom could always read me. And she was full of so much life."

"She did love you." Judy looked out the window. "It was less complicated between you two."

"Remember how she used to call me Bogart?"

"How could I forget? For some reason you reminded her of Humphrey." Judy looked out the window. "*Maltese Falcon* was her favorite movie."

"Yeah, I remember." My dad paused and then continued, "So I was thinking that maybe I would call the puppy Bogart but that sounded too . . . I don't know . . . too much. Then I thought that I could shorten it to Bo but all I could think about was Bo Derek in that stupid Dudley Moore movie. And then it came to me, Beau. I looked it up. It means an attentive male companion."

"I think it also means a male escort." Judy chuckled and patted my head. "I think it's perfect."

"You do?"

"Yeah, he seems like a Beau. And it's a nice tribute to my mom. Thanks."

"I'm glad you like it. I'm thinking about having a puppy shower. What do you think?"

"Could be fun. Would you invite my brother and the kids?" Judy asked.

"Sure. The kids would love Beau."

Judy caressed my back. "When's the last time you saw them?"

"I ran into them in Golden Gate Park a month or so ago," my dad replied.

"Really?" Judy's eyebrows moved up. "John didn't tell me."

"Oh, sorry."

"It's OK, my brother never tells me anything." Judy shrugged her shoulders. "They're your godkids too."

"I can't believe how much they've grown. They're so different. Adrian's so quiet and shy, and Julian can't stop talking."

"I know. I have to always remind myself to pay attention to Adrian. You know it's the quiet ones you have to worry about. You were a quiet one, weren't you?"

My dad nodded his head. "Yeah, I guess so. It was better in my own private world."

"The quiet ones always look self-sufficient."

"Things aren't always as they appear. Adrien is lucky to have you." My dad smiled a sad smile.

Judy brightened. "So, the party should be fun."

"Yeah, I think so too. I'm going to invite Anthony."

Judy groaned.

"I wish you two would try to get along."

"He just gets on my nerves. It always feels like he's gloating."

"No, he's not."

"He's always been that way, competitive. When we were at Stanford together it used to be fun, him and me against the world. But now it feels like he's always competing with me."

"Well, I wish you'd try again." My dad smiled. "Do it for Beau, he needs both of his aunties."

"HEY ANTHONY," my dad said into the talking-machine.

"Do you have plans on Sunday?"

"Great, I'm having a puppy shower for Beau."

"Oh, that's right. I forgot to tell you. I named the little guy."

"I know that it took me forever but I wanted to get it right. Judy's mom inspired his name. You know she used to call me Bogart. I just shortened it to Beau."

"Yeah, she was an incredible woman."

"For the record, you used to think Judy was incredible too."

"I'm not taking sides. It takes two. Anyway, Beau reminds me of Claire. Beau knows things. He's an old soul."

"I thought I'd invite a few people from work, Judy's brother and family, and my neighbor Mrs. Harris."

"Mrs. Harris had me over the other day. We're an unlikely pair but I like her, even with her churchiness. I didn't know she had a son who died. He died of AIDS in the '80s."

"I know. I think everyone in this city has some AIDS connection."

"The party's at 2:00."

"Of course Judy is coming, and you WILL be nice!"

"Sure, bring whoever you want."

"What's his name, I mean how old is he? Never mind, but how close is he to your dad's age?" My dad started chuckling.

"OK, I'll stop. I look forward to meeting him."

"Gifts? Sure, but skip Tiffany's and just go to Petco. If Beau can't chew it, it's of no use."

"Great, see you Saturday. Bye."


MY DAD SPENT the next several days in a constant state of movement, most of it not including me. He bustled around, moving things, hiding things, and replacing all the good smells with things that made me sneeze. The worst was that awful machine that made a whirling, sucking noise. Its body rolled on wheels and it had a long, skinny neck. When I tried to smell it, it grabbed my nose and tried to suck my whole head into its mouth. Needless to say, we didn't become friends. I moved on to a chewable chair leg, the strings on the end of the rug, the stuff in the floor baskets that needed to be sorted: edible treats from the plastic wrappings, papers, and bottles. My dad never seemed happy with my activities, but he didn't have any better ideas. He just kept yelling at me and going about his business without me. It wasn't like him. A change in human behavior can never be ignored. Something was going to happen. And sure enough, the day of the gathering the world got bigger and more exciting.

Every time the doorbell rang, a new surprise appeared. Every set of legs brought something different. First Judy bounced in, bare legs under a tight tent, heels clicking as she walked. She bent low enough for my nose to brush her lips.

"Hello, sweet pea."

I wiggled. My hindquarters wobbled faster than the rest of my body and I fell onto my back, legs in the air.

"Give me that little belly." Judy patted and gritted her teeth. "Beau, such a sweetie, yes you are."

My dad watched and smiled. "I don't know why he always ends up on his back for you."

Judy stood up and gave my dad a kiss. "He's not stupid. He knows what side his bread gets buttered." She handed a package to my dad. "Here's something to welcome him to the family. Open it before everyone gets here."

"OK." My dad pulled off the paper. "Wow, when did you take this picture of Beau? I remember this one of your mom."

"Aren't they great?" Judy smiled.

"They're wonderful. I love both of them. I love that they're in the same frame. Thank you." My dad gave Judy a hug. "It's perfect." My dad lowered the picture to the floor. "Look, Beau, it's your grandma."

The doorbell rang again. When my dad opened the door, Mrs. Harris stood at the door smiling with a bag that leaked savory smells.

"Hello little one, Beau, is it? What a sweet name. And yes, this is for you."

I jumped up to get a better sniff.

"Hello, Ben." Mrs. Harris gave my dad a hug and then held up the bag. "*The Today Show* had a show on homemade doggie treats. I wrote down the recipe. They're made with peanut butter and bananas. I thought they sounded good enough to eat." Mrs. Harris chuckled. "But I hope your puppy likes them more than I did."

"That's so sweet of you, thank you, Mrs. Harris." My dad held his hand toward Judy. "You remember Judy."

"Yes, of course." Mrs. Harris offered her hand to Judy. "Nice to see you, dear."

"Hello, Mrs. Harris, good to see you too. I love your hat."

"Thank you, honey, it's the secret of a good hat, covers up hair that's not acting right." Mrs. Harris' eyes twinkled.

"Come on in." My dad gestured down the hall. "There's food and drinks in the kitchen."

As everyone walked down the hallway, the doorbell rang again. I did a quick reverse.

"I'll get it," Judy announced and followed me to the door.

When she opened the door, Anthony stood at the door with his arm around a large man with lots of whiskers.

"Oh, hi Judy, this is Mark." Anthony quickly bent down and chased me with his hand. "Always ready to play, hey Beau, how are you, buddy?" He looked up at his furry friend. "Isn't he cute?"

I ran circles around both of them.

Judy held out her hand. "Hi, Mark, I'm Judy. Come on in."

"Nice to meet you." Mark shook Judy's hand.

"Is Ben in the kitchen?" Anthony nudged Mark past Judy. "He's an amazing cook."

Judy stepped aside and then looked out the door at a small group at the bottom of the stairs. "And you all must work with Ben. Come on in. I'm Judy." They all shook her hand and filed into the house.

Before I had the chance to follow them, a little human came bounding up the stairs.

"Hi, Auntie Judy," he squeaked.

Two big humans stood at the bottom of the stairs with another little-one peaking out from behind their legs.

Judy grabbed the little-one running up the stairs and hugged him tight.

"Hi, Julian, are you ready to meet the puppy?" She put him on the ground, and I jumped and licked. His face and shirt were filled with flavors. "This is Beau. Beau, this is Julian." Julian was perfect. Unlike the big humans he couldn't get up and leave me on the floor. I was dizzy with all the play possibilities right before my nose. Judy suddenly interrupted, "Wait a minute, Julian, don't you have a brother?"

The little-one looked up at Judy and giggled.

She continued, "Hey, did you leave your brother at home." Judy looked down the stairs at the humans. "John and Bonnie, did you leave Adrian in the car? I wonder where he could be."

"Here I am, Auntie Judy." The little-one behind the legs suddenly jumped forward.

"Did I hear something? John, I swear I just heard Adrian's voice."

Julian pointed down the stairs. "Auntie, Adrian's down there."

"Oh my gosh, you're right. Adrian, you better get up here and give your Auntie a kiss."

The second little-one didn't make it to Judy's arms. I cut him off and instead of squealing he just sat down. I jumped into his lap. His clothes smelled fresh without hints of food. He looked at me with wide eyes. His pudgy hands rubbed me softly.

"Adrian, this is Beau. I think he likes you."


ONCE THE BELL stopped ringing, everyone got busy eating. I ate all the droppings that fell to the floor. In between cleanup, I spent time with the little-ones. Julian ran through the house in a wild game of chase. When his excitement wore out, I found Adrian's quiet lap. He whispered things in my ear that I didn't understand, but I loved the feel of his face next to mine. He didn't try to pull away but let me inhale the sweet smell of young human flesh.

At some point everybody started to leave, leaving only Anthony and Judy. They avoided each other most of the day, but then it was just the two of them, standing in the eating-room staring down the hallway, waiting for my dad. Anthony shifted from one foot to the other, and Judy had her arms crossed. They looked like they needed something to do. I ran, got my ball, and dropped it at their feet. They ignored me but both relaxed when my dad walked into the room.

"It was really a nice party, Ben. What a nice diverse group," Judy said.

Anthony looked at Judy. "Guess it's a relief that Ben still has straight friends?"

Judy shook her head, "You're so predictable. Why does everything have to be about sexual preference?"

"Well, maybe because you always bring it up. And for the record, it's not a preference, that is unless YOU just happen to prefer the opposite sex."

"It's always about you, Anthony! It was a diverse party — kids, men, women, all colors. The world isn't just gay and straight. Get over it."

"Stop it." My dad looked like he might make them do a sit. "You both were good today. I appreciate it. Don't ruin the sweet taste. Can I make you to-go plates? I'll never eat all these leftovers."

Judy and Anthony both took deep breaths.

Judy replied, "Sure, that would be great. That cake was amazing. I'd love a piece for my lunch tomorrow."

Anthony turned his head and rolled his eyes.

Judy's body became stiff. "What, like you're some dainty flower who doesn't eat cake? You're such a priss."

"Girl, you just might want to watch those hips."

"You're one to talk. You think that if you wear clothes that are too small, you're going to shrink. You have more junk in your trunk than I'll ever own."

"Buttercup, it's called glutes, as in muscle."

"Darlin', it's called wishful thinking, as in denial."

I watched Judy and Anthony throw their words back and forth. I got my tug rope so I could play too. I was just about to clunk Anthony's ankle with the rope.

My dad banged on a pot and made my ears tingle. "That's enough," he shouted.

Excited, I dropped my tug and ran over to my dad and danced around his feet.

"Although I have some morbid curiosity about what would happen if I left you two to your own devices, I don't want to clean up the mess. I love you both too much to watch you fight without a referee." He banged on the pot again. "This round is OVER. Here's your goodie bag, Judy."

I started to jump up on my dad. The bag smelled incredible.

My dad put his arm around Judy. "Thanks for the great gift. Let's have dinner next week." I followed as they walked to the front door. Anthony stayed in the eating- room.

At the front door Judy kissed my dad on his cheek. "Bye, hon. I'm glad Beau found you."

My dad hugged back. "Bye, Judy, thanks for coming."

As Judy opened the door, Anthony yelled from the eating-room, "Good-bye, Judy, always a pleasure."

Judy shouted back, "Just like a root canal!" She walked out and closed the door.

My dad stood quietly and looked at the door. I wondered if he was waiting for Judy to come back. I barked so she would. She didn't. We walked back to the eating- room.

"Well, that went well." Anthony was smiling with all his teeth.

My dad held out his fist, and only the middle finger was standing up.

Anthony laughed. "It was a great party, Ben. Beau's a hit."

Anthony picked me up. I pushed one side of my head and then the other into his hand as he rubbed. The inside of my ears were always hot and itchy. I tried to shake 'em, scratch 'em, and rub 'em, but human hands did things that I couldn't. My breathing turned heavy as Anthony discovered my spot.

"It was a fun party," my dad agreed.

Anthony's hand continued to roam my ears. "I didn't want to bring this up when Judy was here but can you believe that whole Andrew Cunanan story? He used to live in San Francisco! He used to hang out with the rich Pacific Heights crowd. I know guys who knew him!" Anthony shook his head. "I can't believe Versace is dead."

"It's crazy. And of course the media loved that rumor that Cunanan went on a murder spree because he had just found he was HIV positive." My dad started to stack dishes.

"Thankfully, the autopsy proved that rumor false." Anthony added.

My dad turned on the water. "I know there are crazy gays in the world but I hate when they make the news."

Anthony nodded his head. "That's the problem with being a minority. Society never thinks that a straight, white man does something crazy *because* he's straight, white and male."

My dad put the dishes in the water. "Sorry your date had to leave so early. I hardly had a chance to talk to him."

"He got paged and had to go into work . . . the life of a surgeon. I thought it would be sexy dating a doctor but the hours suck. So, what about you?"

My dad sighed. "Not good. I'm still doing the AOL chat rooms, even though it never works out."

Anthony stopped rubbing. "So why do you continue?"

"It's convenient. It's there."

"So what's the problem?"

"Everyone just wants sex."

I took a little nip of Anthony's hand. "Ouch, stop that." He started to rub again. "And that's a problem?"

"I want to get to know someone first, BEFORE I meet his private parts."

"But you're online!"

"So . . .? My profile says I want to date."

"Please, I've seen your pic. Don't you think it's a bit of a mixed message?"

"No, I want them to think that I'm sexy."

"And then what? I think you are walking a fine line; besides, sex can lead to more."

"I know."

"Don't be so uptight! You used to love sex."

"That's the problem. The idea is exciting but the doing isn't. I'm not the same person."

Anthony sighed. "Ben, you *are* the same person. All these people here today see the same person today that they've always seen."

My dad looked away. "But they don't know."

Anthony cradled me in his big arm. "Maybe it's time to tell some of them. The only power of a secret is the power we give it."

I sank deeper into Anthony's flesh and closed my eyes, full, happy, and sleepy.

# Chapter 7

## No Yes No

My eyes were half open. It was my favorite time of day. After a good morning stroll and the crispy crunch of breakfast, everything was right—no pee, no poop, and a full belly. The day was bright with sunshine. I snuggled into my pillow and curled into a ball, my eyes heavy from the warmth streaming through the window and the slow thump inside my chest.

"Hey Anthony," my dad said into the talking-machine. "How's it going?"

"What are you doing on Sunday?"

"It's Beau's first day of puppy school."

"No, I'm not kidding. He needs to socialize. He really hasn't been around any dogs. We had to wait until he was done with all his vaccinations."

"Yeah, it's as much for us as for the puppies. They say we're the ones that need to learn."

"That's the truth. Lord knows there're a bunch of parents at my school that could use some class time. Maybe we should take a page from doggie education."

"Can you imagine a room full of puppies?"

My eyes were almost closed. The low vibrations of my dad's voice buzzed gently in my ear.

"I thought your Shanti client was on Saturdays." There was unexpected silence. I opened my eyes slightly. My dad was staring at the ceiling.

When he spoke his voice was lower. "I'm sorry. I thought he was doing better."

"I don't know how you do it? Where's his family?"

"They don't know? How could they not know? He's in an AIDS hospice!"

"Those public health campaigns always say that AIDS can happen to anyone, but that's a lie." My dad sounded mad. "The reality is that if you're a drug user or a homosexual, you have a much better chance of winning the prize. If your Shanti client was a hemophiliac he'd be a victim and his parents would wear a red ribbon like a badge of honor. Victims are good people caught in a bad situation. That doesn't apply to druggies or sodomites."

"Am I bitter? Ah, yeah, 'Bitter . . . party of one.' Remember when we first saw *Rent*? We couldn't believe that our stories were on Broadway. We thought it would change people's perceptions, but people don't really change. 'Seasons of Love' is just a sentimental Broadway tune."

My dad sighed and the talking stopped.

"Yeah, I'm still here. I should get going. Wish you could go with us, maybe another time."

"OK, bye."

I heard the clunk of the talking-machine. My dad sat and stared. The air was heavy with quiet. My head sunk deeper into my pillow.

I woke up to talking. "Hey, Judy," my dad said into the talking-machine. "What are you doing?"

"Yeah, it's hot. It's kind of early for Indian summer. It doesn't usually start in August."

"I know you hate it." My dad paused, "What are you doing Sunday?"

"Really?" My dad found his happy voice. "Want to go with me and Beau to puppy kindergarten?"

"I'm not sure but I think about twenty other puppies."

"I know. Doesn't it sound like fun? It'll be pure pandemonium. We could have lunch after."

"Great. I'll pick you up at 9:30. The class is on 18th Street in the Mission District. The class goes until noon."

"Cool. Thanks Judy, I really appreciate it. See you Sunday."


I DON'T KNOW how humans know where they are going without keeping track of where they've been. My nose is my guide. I always smell my way, but in four-wheels the smells either never change or change too fast.

The sun was hot. No matter how far I let my tongue hang down, I didn't feel any cooler. My dad opened the back door to four-wheels, and I jumped in. The air inside four-wheels wrapped me in hot blankets, and I felt like I couldn't breathe.

The usual sweet smell under my dad's arms was pushed aside by sour funk.

"Wow, it's a hot one. You must be dying, Beau. Hold on, the AC will kick-in in just a minute."

As we started to roll, I felt a waft of cool drift over my dad's shoulder. Relieved but exhausted, I plopped down and stretched out long and let my eyes go droopy. Who knew where we were going, but it was too hot to care. Sometime later I was startled by the sound of an opening door. I felt the rush of hot air.

"Hi, Judy," my dad said with a big smile.

Judy was wearing mostly skin. I like when humans wear skin. Clothes make them smell like they're hiding something. I tried to climb over the seat to get closer.

"Whoa, little man, take it easy. Here, let me give you some love." Judy turned and brought her face close to my nose. I licked her nose and then went for her ears. She started laughing but pushed me back so my tongue couldn't reach her face. "There. Smell all you want, but let's save the licking for all the puppies you're going to meet."

"I can't compete with that hello. How are you?" my dad said as his hands firmly grasped four-wheels and we rolled away.

"About ready to melt. We're supposed to still be socked in fog. It's going to be even hotter in the Mission. Do you think they'll have air conditioning?"

"I called, and they said that they have air."

"Good."

Suddenly a new smell arrived in four-wheels. I checked the windows but they were still closed. I sniffed my butt, and it wasn't coming from me.

Since I was down there, I paused to give my pee-pee a quick wash. Well, it always starts out quick but then feels better than I remember so I stay longer.

"Yewww. Beau, is that you?" Judy put her hands over her nose. "Wow, he can sure put out some gas."

"Yeah, he's got vicious farts." My dad looked guilty as he rolled down the windows and hot air poured in.

"Ugh, not sure I like the heat any better." Judy wrinkled her nose. "Roll the window back up."

It was slow going as we rolled past cars and buildings. More humans than usual were out on the streets. Finally we stopped and when the doors opened, heat streamed in again. I jumped over the seat and out the door.

"Just a minute, mister." My dad attached the leash.

We walked down a sidewalk, and there were dog smells everywhere. My tail started to shake my whole body. My dad stopped at a door. I could hear lots of barking. Someone was scared, someone was having fun, and someone was going to start a fight.

My dad pushed a button by the door.

"Hi, can I help you?" a muffed voice came from a box next to the door.

My dad leaned toward the door. "Yes, we're here for the puppy class."

"Oh, great, I'll buzz you in. Go through the first gate and make sure it latches. Then come on in through the second gate. We don't want any puppies on the loose."

I raced through the door.

My dad suddenly stopped. "Judy, could you take Beau. I have to do something." He handed Judy the leash and quickly walked away.

"Uh, sure Ben . . . just leave me alone." Judy looked down at me and shook her head. "Well, let's go, big guy, it's time to meet your peeps."

We went through the two gates, and suddenly I was in a big room full of dogs. No one looked like me. There was big hair, no hair, flat noses, big noses, and so many colors. I had no idea we could be so different. A tan, skinny, long-legged puppy ran over to me. His tail was wagging as fast as mine. He sniffed my nose, backed up, and then sprang toward me. He shook his head and barked. He didn't need to do anymore. I took off and the leash flew out of Judy's hand.

"Wait, come back here. Beau, stop." Judy ran after me as I ran after Legs.

As we ran past a little white fluffy puppy, she ducked behind her human's legs and hid. A bossy, black-and-white puppy with a stub tail started chasing us, barking at us to slow down. He even tried to take a little nip at my heels. A black curly-haired puppy tried to join the chase but kept running into things. Legs and I eventually stopped to catch our breath. A small, short-haired puppy watched us with bulging eyes. He made a low growl. I cocked my head sidewise. Next thing I knew he jumped out of his human's lap and headed straight for me and snapped. I dropped, belly to the floor, and yelped.

Judy ran over and picked me up. "Beau, are you OK?"

"Is that your dog?" the woman scolded. "He's instigating."

"Are you kidding me?" Judy put her hands on her hips. "Your dog attacked him."

"Try to control your dog." The human walked away with Big Eyes.

"Bitches, both of them," Judy whispered under her breath. She looked around the room. "Where's your dad? I don't know what I am supposed to do here?"

I saw my dad walking toward us. I wiggled out of Judy's arms.

"Where have you been?" Judy said sternly. "I had to break up a fight and that woman over there yelled at me."

My dad smelled like he had been to a water-room.

"Sorry, thanks for watching him. I can't believe Beau would be in a fight."

"It wasn't Beau's fault. That prissy little thing started it. But where the hell did you go?"

Suddenly there was a loud whistle. "OK, class, let's get started." The human with the whistle was standing in the middle of the room. "Let's put your dogs on their leashes and get in a semi-circle."

All the humans called their dogs. Some offered treats and sweet voices. Others wagged their fingers and used loud sharp words. Eventually we all heard the "clink" and felt the leash snap into place. We all sat in a big circle. Well, the humans sat. Most of us dogs just couldn't.

"Welcome, everyone. Our goal today is to make this fun for you and your puppy," the human in the middle of the room announced.

"Beau, sit still," whispered my dad.

I pulled to get closer to Legs.

"Beau, SIT." My dad reached into his pocket and gave me a soft smoky treat.

The human in the middle continued, "All dogs love to please. Training your puppy will be easy if you keep it positive and fun."

I could smell that my dad had more treats. He sat tall and stared at the human that was talking. I pushed my nose into his pants' pocket.

"Stop it!" my dad hissed.

I started to scratch and dig in his pocket.

Judy leaned toward my dad and whispered, "Got any extra hot dogs?"

She put her hand over her mouth and snorted. Her whole body started to jiggle. My dad's face turned red.

"Shut up, Judy," he said with tight lips and stared straight ahead.

"OK, class, I'm going to keep my lectures short. We're going to learn by doing. The first thing we'll work on is the command SIT."

Judy leaned forward again. "That sounds like a great place for you guys to start."

Her eyes sparkled with fun. I jumped into her lap and my tongue headed for her face.

"Stop it, you two! Beau, get back here!" My dad pulled me out of Judy's lap.

"OK, everyone find a spot in the room where you and your puppy can work. Spread out so your puppy won't be distracted. This would be a good time to take out those treats I asked you to bring."


"THAT WAS FUN." Judy put her arm around my dad as we walked toward the door.

"Yeah, it was," my dad nodded. "How do you think Beau did? I mean, compared to the others?"

Judy shook her head. "Relax, he did great. But I hate to be the one to tell you, old man, I think your kid is wired for fun and not college." Judy laughed and bent down and ruffled my hair.

Once outside, the heat made everything slow down. But in the distance I heard the sound of water.

My dad pointed to a park. "Do you mind if we make a quick stop before we get in the car? Beau probably needs a bathroom-run."

I pulled toward the great big grassy field. At one end it was raining.

"Don't get any ideas, Beau, no sprinklers for you."

My dad kept me in the dry area. The grass had lots of pee spots, and I explored as many as I could. Judy and my dad were busy talking. All of a sudden there was movement in the grass, and something rose from the ground. There was a putter and then a whirl of water.

"What the . . ." Judy shouted.

"Shit, it's the sprinklers. RUN," my dad shouted back.

Judy covered her head. "Not my hair! I just got it done." She ran to get away.

I love wet surprises. I danced and rolled in the grass.

My dad yanked the leash. "Come on, dammit."

My dad dragged me through the flying rain. When we got to four-wheels, he opened the back door and didn't wait for me to jump. He picked me up and pushed me into the back seat. Then he and Judy got into their seats and slammed their doors.

"I'm soaked. Nothing's dry . . . nothing!" Judy said with big loud breaths. Her face had long dark streaks from her eyes down to her chin. Her hair was dripping.

I gave a big shake that started from my tail and moved up my body to my head. Water flew everywhere.

"NO," Judy and my dad screamed together.

I tried to climb over the seat.

"NO, STAY, NO." Judy and my dad put up their arms and pushed me back into my seat.

They looked at each other, breathing hard. They didn't say anything, chests puffing up and down. All of a sudden they both started to laugh, slow bursts at first and then fast, shoulder-shaking shouts. I pushed past their arms and leaped into the front seat. They laughed harder and louder and started to breathe in loud gasps. I jumped from lap to lap, licking anything I could taste. The water changed us—spicy hair, musky fur, salty skin, and sour clothes.

BACK AT OUR house, wetness dried and gone, my dad and Judy headed straight for the eating-room.

"Let's have some lunch," my dad announced.

It didn't take long for the chopping to turn into wonderful smells. My dad was busy at the counter and Judy sat at the table. I dropped my orange-and-blue ball at Judy's feet and then raced over to my dad to look for fallen treats.

Judy picked up the ball and threw it into the next room. I watched the ball fly through the air, looked back at my dad's feet, and then back at the ball's first bounce. Sometimes life has too many good choices.

"Get it, Beau," Judy said with excitement.

I raced after the ball and cornered it against the wall. I ran back with it squishing in my mouth and then dropped it at Judy's feet.

"I really had fun this morning." Judy turned toward my dad. "We used to laugh like that. Remember our wedding reception?"

"Yeah, and it's always more funny when it's not supposed to be funny," my dad said from the counter.

I carefully watched Judy and the ball, waiting for the chase.

"I thought I was going to have pee stains on my wedding dress. Somehow even that was hysterical," Judy chuckled.

"We did have some good times," my dad said as he carried food to the table.

"And some not so good," Judy said with a sigh.

My dad continued to move things to the table.

"The good times were great, and the bad times were really hard," Judy continued.

"How about we just remember the good." My dad sat down at the table.

They began to eat. I criss-crossed the floor under the table looking for treats.

After some time, Judy cleared her throat. "I miss this." She looked down at me. "Dogs are amazing. Even when they aren't happy, they look like they're expecting happy."

"No begging, Beau." My dad got up and went to my treat drawer. "Here, how about a puppy chew?"

He returned with a snack and I began my sloppy chews. Above me there were the sounds of humans eating, clank of metal, scraping, chewing, clang of glass.

"By the way, Ben, where did you go this morning when you left me with Beau?" Judy asked.

"Nowhere."

"I don't care if you were cruising some guy. I'm just curious."

My dad didn't respond.

"No really, what's the big deal? I just wondered where you went in such a hurry."

My dad shook his head. "It's nothing like that."

"Well, what then?" Judy persisted.

My dad stopped eating. "I had to find a bathroom. I don't want to talk about it."

"Why?" Judy wrinkled her face.

My dad looked away. "Not today, Judy."

# Chapter 8

## Doors

I woke up with a jolt, nighttime quiet shattered.

"BEEP, BEEP, BEEP."

I no longer slept in my house with bars. I had a new pillow on the open floor next to my dad's bed. It was soft and cushy, and the insides smelled like fresh chopped trees. I could stretch out on the massive pillow in any direction without ever touching the floor. I loved the freedom, but I missed the smells of my house. They reminded me of things, things I didn't really remember but knew that I used to know. Everything always changes. I was changing. My body was finally catching up to my ears and paws. It was strange how quickly change becomes normal.

"BEEP, BEEP, BEEP."

I jumped up and ran around my dad's bed, barking. He rolled over. The beeping continued. My dad pushed back the blankets and looked at the beeping white light on the table next to his bed.

"Shit."

He reached over and banged the glowing light. The beeping stopped. He slid back under his blankets. My paws clicked across the hard floor and I returned to my pillow. My dad's breathing got slower. I closed my eyes.

"BEEP, BEEP, BEEP, BEEP, BEEP."

This time I ran straight to the beeping light just in time to see my dad's hand slap the noisemaker so hard that it flew off the table and crashed on the floor.

"NOOO," he groaned.

I reached up and put my nose in his face. He petted my head.

"I don't want to go to work. Where did the summer go? I want to stay home with you."

I sniffed his mouth.

The morning is the best time to smell humans. It's when you can smell who they truly are. During the day they put so many things in their mouths that hide or change their real smell. In the morning you get the full blast of their insides.

My dad's breath was changing. It was starting to smell more metal-like. My dad sighed and slowly slid out of his bed. Even though it was still dark, he acted like it was morning. My tail gathered speed. I had no idea I could have breakfast before the sun woke up. I stayed close to my dad's shuffling feet.


"GOOD BYE BEAU. You don't have any idea what's happening, do you? Anthony will come by later. Be a good boy." My dad carried a bag over his shoulder.

He started to walk toward the door and I ran after him. He stopped and turned around.

"You can't go with me. You have to stay home."

He bent down and held my head in his hands, "I'm gonna miss you, little guy." He quickly stood up. "I gotta go."

He walked out the door. I heard his keys jingle, the click, the sound of his steps and then silence. He had left me home alone before, but this felt different. I could feel it in the way he rushed through the morning, I could see it in the way he packed his bag and in the way he said good-bye. I sat and stared at the door.

I listened carefully for footsteps to return. There was nothing. After a long time of nothing, I wandered through the house looking for him. I looked in the eating-room, no new smells. I checked the sleeping-room, no bed squeaks. I ran into the sitting-room, no talking-boxes. I went back to the front door and waited. Nothing. I wasn't interested in looking for treats. I didn't feel like playing ball. I couldn't bark. I went to my pillow and collapsed.

Some time later, I woke up to sounds at the door.

I jumped up and ran to the front door. Papers were falling through the flap in the door. I didn't even bark. It was just the paper-man. I stared at the papers on the floor. My dad always picked them up before I could check them out, but I wasn't even interested. Then I heard voices outside.

"How's it going?"

"Fine. Thank you. Beautiful day, huh?"

"Yeah, on days like this I love being the mailman."

I heard footsteps moving down the steps. I heard footsteps moving up the steps.

"Well, you have a good day."

"You too."

Suddenly the flap in the door opened.

"Hello in there, anybody home?"

I barked and scratched at the door.

"Hold on, little boy. Where did I put that key?"

My tail wagged faster. The door opened a crack. I tried to wiggle through the opening.

"Whoa, back up, wild child." Anthony slid through the door.

I ran up and down the hallway.

"Wow, and I'm the one that just had a double espresso," Anthony laughed.

He sat down on the floor. "Come here, cutie."

I flew through the air and landed in his lap. I licked everything. Anthony's big hands held me close to his face. His breath was sharp and bitter.

"Hey, you," his fingers gently rubbed under my chin, "how's it being all alone? Trust me, your dad would rather be here than trying to convince teenagers that graffiti isn't art."

He got up and started to walk around the house. He went into the sleeping-room and opened drawers and looked in the closet. He pulled out some clothes.

"What was your dad thinking? Wait a minute . . . this isn't bad. I could wear this."

He looked inside the clothing.

"No wonder, I gave this to him," he chuckled.

I barked and then ran toward the front door.

"OK, OK, we'll go for your walk, just a minute. I've got to see what your dad is up to."

Anthony moved into the water-room. I followed. He started looking in the drawers. He took out several bottles that rattled.

"Videx . . . Viramune . . . here they are . . . Saquinavir . . . Norvir. At least he's taking the new meds. He doesn't tell me anything. He makes me sneak around. Hate to break it to you, pup, but your dad's got some issues."

I whined.

"OK, OK, we're going, we're going." Anthony got my leash and followed me to the door.


AFTER ANTHONY left I went back to bed. My dad was still missing. I woke up when the sunlight was starting its change. The light was soft with hints of red. I was hungry. I went to my empty food bowl. I looked for treats in the usual hiding places. I found one hard crumb under the table. Suddenly, I stopped and stood still. I heard the familiar jingle and sprinted to the door. The door opened as I did my best happy dance. My dad busted through the door without stopping. He ran right past me, huffing and stiff-legged. He went straight to the water-room and slammed the door.

"SHIT."

My dance step slowed to a walk. I heard clothes rustling and the clank of the water-room chair. I sat down and glared at the door.

I cocked my ears. My dad was groaning.

"Ohhhh, ewww," my dad moaned.

I sniffed. A putrid smell came under the door. I barked and pushed on the door with my nose, but it wouldn't open. My dad got quiet and then I heard running water. The water poured down for a very long time. The house was getting darker.

When the door finally opened, a cloud of warm wet smoke poured out. My dad was pink and wrapped in a towel. The sick smell was gone and replaced by sweet flowers.

"Hey, Beau," my dad said softly as he stooped and rubbed my ears. "What a day!"

I started to wiggle. After all day looking and waiting, my dad was finally home. I ran and got my orange-and-blue ball and dropped it in front of him.

The talking-machine started to ring. My dad didn't move. There was a beep and then a familiar voice.

"Hi, Ben, it's Judy, how was your first day back at school? How are the rugrats? Any budding Picassos this year? How did Beau do? Give me a call. Kisses."

I picked up the ball, shook my head, and then dropped it again.

"I don't feel like playing," my dad said.

He sat down and patted his lap. "Come here, come here, Beau."

I picked up the ball and dropped it in his lap.

"No, I don't want to play ball. I said come here."

I crouched low and waited for the ball to fly in the air. My tail was moving fast.

The talking-machine rang again, followed by the beep.

"Hey, Ben, it's Anthony, give me a call. Want to hear about your day and give you the Beau update."

My dad jumped up and ran to the talking-machine.

"Hello . . . hello . . . Anthony?"

"Sorry about that. Just got out of the shower."

"It sucked. I think I'm losing my touch. I used to be excited about the beginning of the school year. I loved when kids used art to express the things they couldn't talk about—the way they looked at their art with surprise and awe, like they were kittens and couldn't believe they had just coughed up a hairball. Now they just seem like angry little people who are always looking for weaknesses so they can swoop in like vultures and peck away. I feel like I'm their prey or maybe the zookeeper."

"Maybe it's just the first day."

"How did it go with Beau?"

"Yeah, I bet he was happy to see you."

"I hope he didn't mess up your afternoon nap. I don't know how you do the night shift. I suppose your patients are cuter when they're sleeping or at least less crazy."

"Really? I'm surprised. I would think there would never be an empty psych bed in this city."

"Yes, you told me about the hot new psychiatrist. This is what happens when you have too much down time. You need to be busy or you get into trouble."

I circled my dad's feet. I wanted to play. I had waited all day.

"Anthony, I don't really want to talk about my day. Let's just leave it alone. Tomorrow's a new day."

"What? You did WHAT?"

"How dare you go through my stuff?"

There was a long pause. My stomach rumbled and reminded me that I was hungry. I started to whine.

"I don't feel like talking about every new drug I'm taking. And for the record, those pills aren't the miracle everyone says they are. Those drugs are causing me hell."

"So what if they save my life if they make me shit on myself like a baby. When's the last time you pooped in your pants? Once we're toilet trained, we're supposed to stay that way!"

"How'd you like worrying about it every time you left the house?"

"That's easy for you to say. You don't have to search for a bathroom when you know you only have seconds."

"It happened today on the way home from work."

"Right, like you'd ever wear diapers!"

"You know what, Anthony? I don't care what you've read or what you've seen. These meds suck, and I'm not sure I'm gonna keep taking them. And next time, stay out of my damn drawers!"

My dad slammed the talking-machine and growled, "Asshole!"

I ran out of the room. I didn't want my dad to throw the talking-machine at me. I watched him from the doorway. He was breathing hard. I whimpered. He turned and looked at me.

"Not you too, what do you want? Leave me alone."

He got up and went to the sleeping-room and closed the door. I didn't know what to do. I didn't know where to sleep. My bed was behind the closed door. My food bowl was empty and it was now dark. I had to pee. I sat and studied the door.

Finally the door opened. My dad stood in the doorway and sighed. He reached down and patted my head.

"Sorry, little one. It's not you. Let's do this."

I ran after him as he opened doors. Soon my pee would splash against a tree, soon I'd be crunching kibble between my teeth, soon I'd be chasing down the ball as it bounced through all the rooms. The only good door is an open door.

# Chapter 9

# Come Go

Four-wheels rolled and whizzed among the other wheels and then slowed to a crawl. It was stop then go and then go and stop. We left the houses and sidewalks behind and were perched high above with water on all sides.

"What a beautiful day," Judy said to my dad. "Good call. I really needed to get out of the city, but we're obviously not alone. This traffic is terrible."

My dad shook his head. "I sure didn't expect the bridge to be like this on a Saturday."

Judy shrugged her shoulders. "That's the Bay Bridge for you. Maybe there's a Raiders game or something? It will be worth the wait."

My dad tipped his head toward me. "It's one of Beau's favorite places."

I pushed my head toward the front seat and Judy reached back and scratched my ears. "Isn't it part of the East Bay Regional Parks? My mom used to take us to Lake Anza when she was dating some schmuck who lived in the Berkeley Hills. We hated him but we loved our outings."

"Speaking of schmucks," my dad smiled, "are you dating?"

"I swore off schmucks, remember?"

"Oh, so you're giving women a test run?"

"Ha-ha, just trying to find a man who's evolved slightly past a Neanderthal."

"How's that going for you?"

Judy frowned. "Not so good. Men can be such dicks, and I do mean that literally and figuratively. Why do you all define yourselves by that stupid appendage that hangs between your legs? Men are so preoccupied with where to put it and how big it is. You'd think it's the epicenter of the universe."

My dad chuckled. "Having some envy?"

Judy bristled. "Never! Freud obviously didn't consult with women when he came up with that stupid penis-envy thing. Truth be told, women think penises are a lot like Tonka trucks — cute, but just toys."

My dad laughed. "Wow, guess I hit a nerve, sounds like someone needs a toy."

Judy reached over and pinched my dad's arm. I tried to climb into the front seat and join the game.

"Whoa, stay back there, Beau." My dad took one hand off the wheel and prevented me from jumping over the seat.

Judy resumed my ear scratching as she looked at my dad. "That's what I'm talking about. Men think sex is the answer to everything."

"Come on, Judy, I was kidding. Believe me, these days I'm with you. Sex is completely overrated."

"Really?"

"Yeah, that's the great myth about gay men—you heteros think we're sex machines. The truth is that most of us are home alone eating popcorn and watching *Will and Grace* with the rest of America."

"So, are you dating?" Judy asked.

"Not really. With Beau, work, and everything else, I don't really have the interest or the time."

"Hmmm." Judy looked out the window.

WE FINALLY STOPPED rolling on a quiet road surrounded by trees.

"Incredible." Judy sighed. "There's something about the light in the fall. With the brown hills, everything looks gilded. We're so lucky to live here."

At the first creak of the door, I bolted outside. My dad grabbed my leash. "Slow down, buster, you're not free until we get on the trail."

I loved this place. No houses on top of houses, just hills covered by bushes and trees, no screech and rumble of wheels, just the chirp of birds and the rustle of the breeze sliding through pine needles. Instead of humans not looking, humans on these trails nodded and smiled.

I stopped at the first tree. The smells were deep. This was older, darker dirt. I lifted my leg and peed. We set off toward freedom. My dad unclicked my leash and I tore off with my nose leading the way. I could hear my dad's and Judy's feet crunch on the fallen leaves and crushed rock behind me. This place didn't have human surprises smashed into the path or hiding in plastic wrappings. The bushes weren't only scented with dog pee but held other mysterious animal smells.

My hind legs felt light, as my nose hurried from smell to smell. A flash of grey and brown darted in front of me, and I set off on a chase.

"Beau . . . Stop, COME HERE," my dad shouted.

My ears bounced and flopped unused as my nose took over.

"Beau, get back here!"

The voice was distant. I leaped over rocks and skidded around bushes and caught another glimpse of the bushy tail. It raced straight up a tree and out of sight. I tried to follow, but my nails slid down the tree and I fell backwards. I barked and ran around in circles.

"Beau, come here NOW." I suddenly heard my dad's voice thundering toward me.

I know what *come* means. And I know that *go* means the opposite. But sometimes when my dad says come it really sounds like go. Human don't always mean what they say. And then sometimes they do.

"Beau, where are you, honey, come to Auntie." Judy's voice floated through the shrub.

I searched for Bushy Tail, but the scent had grown quiet.

"Here, Beau, come to Aunt Judy." Judy's voice was warm and sweet.

I ran to Judy and slid to a stop at her feet.

"There you are, pumpkin." Judy rubbed my back. "Ben, he's over here," she called.

My dad came huffing toward us, red-faced and breathing hard.

"Don't you ever run off like that!"

"He's OK, probably found a squirrel to chase."

"But he is supposed to come when I call. He came when you called. Can you believe that?" My dad stood shaking his head.

"Well, would you come to someone if they were yelling at you?" Judy patted my head and scratched under my chin.

"Beau, come over here!" My dad reached into his pocket and I heard the crackle of plastic. His tone still said go but his pocket said come. My mouth began to fill with saliva. I scampered over to him. "Sure, now you love me."

Judy laughed, "Are you kidding? He's a total papa's boy. He adores you."

My dad gave me the treat. "Let's get back to the trail."

I happily followed as my dad handed out treats every few steps.

"So, how's school going?" Judy asked.

"Awful. Remind me why I teach. I don't think I like it and I'm not very good."

"That's not true. You're a great teacher. But maybe you should get back to your own art too?"

"I sucked at that, too. Don't you remember all those fights about money and getting a real job?"

I zigzagged along the path and looked for more bushy tails but stayed close enough in case my dad handed out more goodies.

"You didn't suck. You just didn't make much money."

"Good artists make money. Bad artists teach middle-school art."

"You can do both. Teach to pay the bills. Do your art to feed your soul."

"I think my soul moved out. He didn't like the company."

"You don't seem very happy."

"Oh, and I used to be so much fun. Remember all our good times."

"Stop it. This feels different."

I ran to my dad. He pulled out another treat. I gobbled it up. The sun was getting high in the sky. My tongue dangled in the warm air. My dad and Judy took off their jackets.

"He's such a great dog. He never seems to run out of wonder," Judy said as she wrapped her jacket around her waist. "Are you losing weight?"

"No." My dad kicked a rock on the path and started to walk faster.

"Are you sure?"

"Yes." He walked past Judy.

"Your face looks thinner."

My dad stopped and turned around. "You always thought I needed to lose weight."

"I was just wondering."

"Your wondering always sounds like something else. Let's go. I want to get to the picnic area." He started walking again.

"Wait up, what's the hurry?"

My dad started walking even faster.

"Ben, stop, what's wrong with you?"

"If you must know, I've got to get the bathroom, OK?" He hurried off in a trot, leaving Judy behind.

It's always exciting when humans run. It almost never happens.


A BLANKET COVERED the grass. Judy and my dad sat on the blanket. They emptied the bags they had carried on their backs. The blanket was filled with savory and sweet smells.

"Off, Beau, get off the blanket." My dad tried to push me away.

I grabbed a soft, creamy chunk and quickly swallowed.

My dad caught me by my collar and led me off the blanket. "Sorry buddy, this isn't for you. Where's your friend in the woods."

"Poor Beau, he just wants to be part of the picnic. Can't he have some prosciutto?" Judy made my tail wag.

"No, he doesn't get people food."

"Look at him. How can you say no to those big, sad eyes?"

"You wouldn't be doing anybody a favor by giving him picnic food. He has terrible farts."

My dad threw a stick into the woods. My tail sped up and I chased the flying toy. I returned with the stick and dropped it next to the blanket.

"I don't know how you can say no to him."

"It's called love."

Judy shook her head. "If only people were so good at accepting no. Look at him. He's already moved on. Now he's excited about a tree branch."

No one threw the stick. I started to chew.

"So, are you OK?" Judy asked as she took a bite of something crunchy.

"What do you mean?"

"You ran off to the bathroom like you were going to be sick."

"Great conversation . . . goes so well with Brie and baguettes."

"I didn't ask for the gory details."

"Oh, so now you don't want to know."

"Ben, you're like trying to hold on to a slippery fish. I think we're about to have a conversation, and then you twist and turn, and before I know it you've slid out of my hands. I just wanted to know if you're OK! I thought it was a basic question, but maybe we should convene a grand jury."

My stick was amazing. Once I chewed through the rough outside, I discovered a smooth and stringy inside. It came apart in strips as I chewed and pulled. The talking stopped. I looked up. My dad turned away from Judy.

Judy pointed her finger at him. "Oh, and don't you dare start to pout. I'm the one that deserves to be irritated, not you."

Something was changing. I got up and walked over to my dad.

"Beau, not on the blanket." I sniffed his face. "Go." He pointed to the grass.

I went back to my stick and watched.

"There's something I should tell you," my dad said slowly.

Judy interrupted, "I really don't want another lecture about how I badger you with questions and beat you down. Let's just drop it."

"No, this time you're right." He took a deep breath. "I need to tell you something."

Judy sat up straighter.

"I probably should have told you sooner, but you know I'm not good at this."

Judy crossed her arms. "OK, Ben, now you're scaring me."

My dad looked down at the blanket. "You know I don't like to talk about stuff."

"Out with it. You don't want to have a sex change, do you?" Judy chuckled without smiling.

My dad was looking down at the blanket like he'd lost something. "I hate this. I know you're going to be mad."

Judy stared without speaking.

"Judy, I've . . . got it." My dad quickly looked at Judy.

Judy's mouth dropped slightly like she was going to talk, but nothing came out.

My dad continued, "You know, the disease."

The color in Judy's face changed. The pink lost its color. Slowly water appeared in her eyes.

My dad watched her and then looked away. "I'm sorry, Judy," he said quietly.

Judy moved over to my dad and laid her head on his shoulder. My dad put his arms around her and they rocked back and forth. I jumped on the blanket and tried to push my head between them. They didn't seem to notice. Judy whimpered. Suddenly she pushed my dad away.

"How could you?" she blurted out.

I jumped into Judy's lap. She ignored me. "Oh Ben, how could you?"

My dad was silent. He didn't move but looked down at me. He held out his hand. I licked it. He scratched my head.

Judy took several deep inhales. Her face was shiny. "I don't know what to say. I know I'll say the wrong thing."

"It's OK. There's nothing to say. What's done is done."

"How long?"

"I don't know."

"But you were negative when we got divorced."

"I did some stupid things after the divorce. I must have gotten it when I was drinking, but I didn't find out until I was in the hospital with alcohol poisoning."

"That was 1992, five years ago. You've known for all this time, and you're just telling me now? Why didn't you tell me? How could you keep this from me?"

"I didn't want to talk about it. I didn't want you to know. It's such a cliché. Gay man comes out, gay man gets AIDS."

"Why are you telling me now?"

"My T cells aren't great, and the meds are making me sick."

"What is it with you and secrets? Your secrets always hurt. I thought we were going to be honest." Judy frowned. "This feels so familiar, same scene, different script."

Judy folded her arms. "Ben, I'm sorry. I can't do this. I don't know what to say. I have too much to say. I have nothing to say."

Silent water rolled down my dad's face.

Judy blew her nose. "I just can't lose you . . . again."

My dad wiped his eyes. "What does that mean, Judy?"

"Let's just go home." Judy pushed me out of her lap and started to put things into her bag.

"OK." My dad started to wrap up food.

I got my stick and dropped it on the blanket.

"No, Beau, not now, we're going home." My dad moved the stick without throwing it.

Judy stood and put her bag on her back. My dad started to pick up the blanket. I slipped and skidded as the blanket lifted into the air. I rolled off the blanket and landed on my back. I quickly jumped up so we could play that one again. The blanket disappeared into my dad's bag. Judy started walking down the path and my dad followed. I ran after them but then ran back for my stick.


I SLEPT ALL the way home in four-wheels. I didn't even hear when Judy was dropped off at her house. When we got home my dad headed straight for the talking- machine. I headed to my pillow and circled twice, plopped down, and watched my dad.

"Hey, Anthony."

"We just got back."

"It didn't go well. Actually, it was terrible."

"She's mad! We didn't talk all the way home from Oakland. What should I do?"

"I don't think time will fix it."

"This feels different. You didn't see the look in her eyes."

"How can you take her side? I'm not the one who is running away. She's the one who said she couldn't do this, whatever that means? And what about me? Did it ever occur to her that I don't want to do THIS either. I certainly don't want to get sick around her. Hell, I don't want to be sick around anyone."

"No, not you either. I just want it like it used to be, when I didn't always think about my health. I hate when I see worry in your eyes—or worse, pity. It's bad enough that it's all I see when I look in the mirror. The other day I was walking downtown at Union Square and I saw someone who I used to teach with. His face had that sunken look, no cheeks, only cheekbones, skin stretched over bones. You know, the AIDS look. He saw me and immediately looked down at the sidewalk. I turned my head. He didn't want to be seen. I didn't want to look. Everyone's tired of looking. Those red ribbons have lost their charm."

"Of course I know you love me."

"Could you talk to Judy? I know she won't talk to her family or friends. Maybe she'll talk to you."

"Thanks. I'm wiped out. I think I'm going to turn in early tonight."

"Love you too."

"Bye."

My dad lay down on the floor. He curled up on his side and looked at me with tired eyes. I got up from my pillow and snuggled into the spot next to his belly. I felt his belly go in and out as his breathing became slow and heavy. I took a deep breath, let it go, closed my eyes, and thought about Bushy Tail. It's always great to go places, and it's always great to come home.

# Chapter 10

# Tug

My dad had two kinds of mornings. During the grumpy ones, he raced out the door fully clothed with his bag draped over his shoulder (when he clearly didn't feel like running) and during the happy ones, he puttered along in his bedclothes and always took time to play with me. I thought it was going to be one of those slow ones until the talking-machine rang.

"Hello," he muttered.

"WHAT? Why are you coming today? Why'd you change your flight?"

"Harvey, I know today is Thanksgiving, but you said you were coming tomorrow."

"Of course it would be nice to spend Thanksgiving together. I just wasn't planning on it. I didn't even buy a turkey."

"No, it doesn't have to be traditional. When has our family ever been traditional?"

"Is she OK with that?"

"Sure, if she doesn't mind making it but I don't know if I can find the seafood today. It is Thanksgiving."

"You have a direct flight from Phoenix?"

"Yeah, if you have frozen seafood, bring it. Call me when your plane gets in."

"There's a line of cabs outside baggage claim."

"Bye." My dad put down the talking machine with a moan.

He rolled over and stopped at the edge of the bed. His head hung off the side and looked down at me.

"Don't give me that look. I wanted to sleep in, but now I've got to get up."

I perked up my ears and my tail started to wag.

"Are you ready for the family? You think I'm no fun . . . wait until you meet my dad. Shirley, on the other hand, is a marshmallow—way too sweet and mostly air. A little bit of either of them goes a long way. But then, you'll probably love them both." He reached down and rubbed the crown of my head. "OK, let's get up. We've got lots to do."

My dad rushed through the morning. When he clicked the leash on for our morning walk, I knew there wasn't going to be time for fun. His body leaned forward and his feet hurried to keep up. At every good smell, he rushed me forward without even a chance to investigate.

There was no nap after breakfast. He didn't stare out the window or rustle through his paper. Instead of ball time, he took out the long-necked-sucker and rolled him through the house, almost running me over. He pushed the fuzzy-on-a-stick and slid him over the hard floors without even giving me a chance to play with its fuzz head. He rubbed and scrubbed the water-room on his hands and knees. He moved like he couldn't see me. Even when I sat in his path, he grumbled and nudged me out of his way. But when the talking-machine rang, he leapt over me and ran to the machine.

Humans and their stupid machines! When a machine comes to life, humans always say yes. It doesn't matter whether it blinks, talks, or rings. When a machine wakes up, humans come running.

"Hello."

"Hey, Anthony, I hoped it was you."

"Cleaning like crazy."

"They're coming early. For some reason, they decided we should have a Thanksgiving dinner. I don't know how they got an early flight. Not sure where this sentimental streak is coming from."

"So you're coming, right?"

"Come on, dinner will be great. Well, you know the food will be good. My stepmom is making gumbo."

"OK, Shirley, then—is that better? I don't call my dad, *Dad*."

"Don't try and figure out my family, I can't. So are you coming?"

"Great. Thank you."

"Did you ever call Judy?"

"Really? Maybe you both will get along better if you're both mad at me. Do you think she is ready to see me?"

"It's a good sign that she's talking to you. I sent her an email and told her that Harvey was going be in town."

"Would you let her know about dinner tonight? She should come. Harvey loves her."

"He likes you too . . . well, kinda. He'd love you more if you had breasts." My dad chuckled.

"Yes, that's true. Shirley loves you. I just don't have the stomach for that kind of smothered-love. It's too much for me, but if it works for you, go for it." My dad chuckled again. "Isn't that ironic? Maybe you and Harvey have the same sweet tooth."

My dad's laugh faded. "Strange that I've known her almost as long as I knew my own mother. I've tried to see her as a mom but I guess I prefer my mothering wrapped in narcissism, depression, and a bottle of gin. Sorry, but family always brings out my cheery side. It's stupid, but whenever Harvey comes for a visit, it always feels like I'm twelve and waiting for him to come home. You know, my mom killed herself on the one day of the week that my dad always played golf. It's almost like she wanted me to find the body. How twisted is that?"

"I dialed 911 and when the police arrived, one of the officers went to the golf course to get Harvey. I don't know how he can still play golf."

"OK, I'll put on my big boy pants. I know I should give them points for showing up now. It *is* something."

"You're going to offer Judy a ride? Really? Wow, now I'm scared. The idea of the two of you on the same team." My dad smiled.

"Thanks again, Anthony. I owe you."

"OK, see you soon. Bye."


THE DOORBELL rang. I thundered down the hallway to the front door. My dad was busy moving around the house. The bell rang again,

again and again. Every time it rang I danced faster and barked louder.

"Just a minute," my dad yelled. "I'm coming."

My dad took a deep breath. The bell rang again.

"I'm coming already!" my dad shouted, and then he pointed his finger at me. "No jumping. I mean it! He won't like it."

He swung the door open. I ran outside and jumped up on the man standing at the door. I looked up his long legs and could barely see his head. He didn't bend down. He didn't say hello. His arms were crossed, and he shifted from foot to foot.

"What took you so long? I have to pee like a racehorse." The long man ran past us.

My dad shook his head. "Hello to you too."

I suddenly realized that there was a woman standing at the bottom of the stairs, dressed in purple from head to toe. I raced down but missed the middle stair. I tumbled down and rolled to her soft purple-and-white striped shoes.

"Goodness, look at this one. You must be Beau." She bent down, and my nose got a blast of ripe, sugary fruit. I sneezed but pushed my nose closer. She held my head and gritted her teeth. "Ohhhh, just look at you. You are a special one." Her blue eyes sparkled, nestled in a wrinkled, bronzed face.

"Hi, Shirley." My dad walked down the stairs. "Yup, this is Beau. Looks like he loves you already."

Shirley stood up and held out her arms. "Come here, sweetie, it's so good to see you." My dad hugged Shirley and she kissed him on his cheek. "Ben, it's been too long. We've missed you."

"Oh, uh, me too," my dad nodded.

"OK, that's better." The long man stood in the doorway. "The internal plumbing doesn't work like it used to. When I've got to go . . . I've got to GO!"

I raced up the steps. My dad slowly followed.

"Hi, Harvey."

My dad and the tall man hugged while turning sidewise. It was quick and looked more like a shoulder bump. I jumped up to attempt a smell.

"Off, Beau," my dad ordered. I continued to jump.

"So, this is the ferocious pooch. I can see the training is going well." The man bent down and patted my back.

"Beau, this is your grandpa," my dad said.

"Grandpa? It's not exactly the grandkid I was hoping for. But let's not get started on that one."

"So, how was your flight?" my dad quickly asked.

"We got stuck sitting next to one of those religious nuts."

Shirley giggled. "Harvey, that's not nice. She was sweet. We had a very nice conversation."

"Thankfully, I missed it. I put on my Walkman and fell asleep to Sinatra. Those people don't need guns. They just keep talking until you surrender or convert." He looked at my dad. "I learned how to ignore them after your mother's constant Bible-thumping."

"Hon, don't be mean. At least they know what they believe." Shirley turned to my dad. "But you know how I love to talk. She even gave me some literature to read." Shirley pulled something out of her bag. "Oh look, it's a cartoon about hell. Isn't that unusual?"

My dad turned to Grandpa and wrinkled his face.

Grandpa shrugged his shoulders. "What can I say, she's a saint."

"Hush," Shirley smiled as she scolded. "Get down here and help a lady with her bags."

Grandpa and my dad went down the stairs. My dad picked up the bags.

Grandpa took Shirley's arm. "Let's see what you've done to the place. I hope you're not one of those dog people that turn your house into a dog pen."

I raced ahead to find my tug rope.

Tug is one of those games that always require someone else to play. The rope only works when someone grabs the other end.

GRANDPA YELLED and clapped as he sat in front of the looking-box. In between shouts he threw my tug rope down the hallway. I ran and got it, but Grandpa didn't know how to play. He just threw it without any time to tug. My dad and Shirley were in the eating-room making food. The doorbell rang. I barked and ran for the door.

"It must be Judy and Anthony. Harvey, get the door." my dad shouted.

I was waiting at the door by the time Grandpa arrived.

"This should be interesting," Grandpa muttered.

Grandpa opened the door. Judy was smiling and holding a white bottle. Anthony held a red bottle and stood tall and stiff behind her. I ran past Grandpa and out the door to Anthony's waiting legs. Of course, he reached down and gave me a rub.

Judy held out her arms toward Grandpa. "Harvey, how are you? You look great. What is with you Walkers? You only get more handsome with age."

"Judy! Flattery will get you everywhere," Grandpa smiled as they hugged.

Anthony held me by my collar and rubbed my head. He watched Grandpa and Judy.

"I've missed you," they both said as they let go.

I ran over to Judy and jumped up.

"Of course, I didn't forget you," Judy said as she knelt down to pet me. "Hello, baby, how's my favorite guy? Harvey, so what do you think of Ben's kid?"

"He's something, that's for sure," Grandpa replied. "He's a handful."

Judy rubbed faster. "Have you ever seen so much happiness and love? I think he's great for Ben. Gives him someone to take care of."

"My ears are burning." My dad was suddenly standing in the doorway. "What are you talking about?" He carefully kissed Judy. "Hi Judy," he paused, "I'm so glad you came. Thank you." He then kissed Anthony. "Hey, Anthony."

Suddenly Anthony and Grandpa made eye contact. "Hello, Mr. Walker," Anthony said with an outstretched hand.

My dad scowled at Grandpa. "Harvey, you remember Anthony."

"Of course, Anthony, how are you?" Grandpa firmly took Anthony's hand.

"I'm fine, and you?" Anthony answered.

"I'm fine, how about you? Grandpa replied.

"I'm good . . . fine." Anthony nodded his head. "Sounds like we both are fine."

Judy stopped rubbing my ears as she watched Anthony and Grandpa. I pushed my head into her chest. She started to rub again and asked, "So Harvey, where's Shirley?"

Anthony quickly replied, "She's probably in the kitchen. Her cooking gives Ben a run for his money."

Grandpa's shoulders relaxed and he smiled. "Yup, she's making her world-famous gumbo."

Grandpa put his arm around Judy. "It's so good to see you," he said as they walked into the house.

Anthony handed my dad his red bottle and whispered, "This is fun. But I think this party might need something stronger than this cabernet. You might want to rethink that sobriety thing."

My dad closed his eyes. "Don't tempt me." He put his arm around Anthony.

I ran after Judy and Grandpa. Anthony and my dad caught up, and we all walked into the eating-room.

"WOW, smells wonderful!" Anthony moved toward Shirley. He had to bend low to hug her. "Hi, Shirley."

"Let me get a look at you." Shirley pushed Anthony back and twirled him in a circle. "You've done something different with your hair."

"No, just shaved the goatee . . . and gained a few pounds."

"Well, you're just a peach." Shirley batted her eyes and then turned to Judy. "Judy, you get more beautiful every time I see you. I still keep your wedding picture on the hutch. You know you'll always be part of the family."

"Thanks." Judy wrapped her arms around Shirley and held on for a long time while we all watched.

"OK, that's enough of the gushy stuff, you know you're among Walkers." My dad made a strange laugh. "Don't we have gumbo to make? You guys get out of the kitchen." My dad pointed at Grandpa and Anthony. "You're no help here. Go watch football."

"Are you watching the 49er game?" Anthony asked Grandpa.

"You mean the Arizona Cardinals game. And yes, our boys are kicking some 49er butt. We just took the lead, recovered a fumble on the five-yard line, and scored."

Anthony moaned. "Glad I missed it. Well, it will just make the Niner comeback all the more sweet."

"I doubt that."

"We'll see."

My dad pushed Anthony and Grandpa. "OUT! We don't want your testosterone in here. This is a kitchen. Get out."

Anthony and Grandpa continued to argue as they moved to the sitting-room. I stayed in the eating-room to wait for fallen treats.

My dad shook his head, "Football! So, Shirley, what do you need?"

"The onions and garlic are sautéed, and I'm about to make the roux. I need someone to cut up the chicken and sausages, and someone to chop the green pepper and slice the okra."

Judy moved closer to Shirley. "I want to watch you make the roux. I hear it's the secret to gumbo. Ben, you can do the chopping. You're good at that."

"Gee, thanks." My dad picked up a knife.

The sound of chopping put me on alert. I paced back and forth and watched the floor. Suddenly there were loud shouts from the sitting-room that made my tail wag.

"YES, that's right, GO, GO," Anthony yelled.

"Get 'em, hit 'em . . . SHIT," Grandpa yelled back.

Anthony was clapping. "That's what I'm talking about."

"Wait a minute," Grandpa shouted. "There's a flag . . . holding. Thata boy! Good call, ref! Good-bye, touchdown."

It became quiet again. Something green landed on the floor, and I quickly ate it.

"Too bad I don't give a rip about football. Maybe Harvey and I would actually have something to talk about," my dad said.

Shirley looked up from the pan she was stirring. "Don't be so hard on your father. He's trying. Do you know he's friendly with Philip, my hairdresser? You should see him and Harvey carry on. Some of the questions Harvey asks him make me blush."

"Yeah, well, why doesn't he ask me?"

I sat and waited for something to fall from the counter. The chopping noises stopped.

Judy cocked her head toward my dad. "Maybe it's because you don't want to give him the answers."

"I suppose I deserve that," my dad said to Judy.

"It does take two to make silence," Shirley added.

The room got quiet again.

Shirley continued, "Perhaps you just need to get better at communication. I was watching *Oprah* the other day, and she had a therapist on the show who said that most relationship problems are really communication problems."

"You watch *Oprah*?" My dad asked.

"I sure do." Shirley put her hands on her hips. "Harvey even watches sometime."

"That's kind of hard to picture." My dad quickly added, "Not you, Shirley, but Harvey."

"I wish you'd give him a chance. It was his idea to come early."

I ran and got my tug and dropped it by my dad's feet.

"Ben, he wants to play." Judy picked up the rope. "Look at him, just waiting for something good to happen." Judy looked hard at my dad. "Ben, everybody here loves you. It's not the easy kind of love, but it's real."

My dad looked at Judy and then down at me. "I think I would rather have easy." He sighed and made a half-smile. "But that gumbo smells like it could fix anything. How about we get the table set so we can eat?"


AT FIRST THERE was little talking, only the clink of glasses followed by slurping and chewing, but in time the chatter returned. I roamed under the table among the human legs and feet. Unexpectedly, Grandpa's hand slipped under the table and hung before my face. His hand smelled smoky. He opened his hand and sitting in his palm was a juicy round wrapped in a chewy skin. I gobbled it up and nudged my head between his legs for more.

He pushed my head away but then returned with another chunk.

When dinner was over the humans sat around the table and talked. I lay down under Grandpa's chair and closed my eyes. I was awakened by a puff of wind that escaped from under my tail.

"OHHH, SHIT," Grandpa yelled.

"Oh my," Shirley held her hand to her face.

"Beau!" Judy and Anthony shouted together and then started to giggle.

My dad waved his hands in the air. "Oh, that's nasty. OK, who gave Beau table scraps . . . Harvey?"

"Well, I couldn't eat those Andouille things. They give me heartburn."

"Great . . . thanks . . . so you give them to Beau? You could've just left them on your plate."

"And waste food?" Grandpa raised his glass and pointed it toward Shirley. "It was delicious, dear." He took a big drink.


I RAISED MY head off my pillow. Light was beginning to uncover the things that had been hiding during the night. I sniffed the morning news. I caught the faint scent of last night's dinner and felt my mouth fill with saliva. I remembered Anthony and Judy leaving, but I was so tired that I didn't even remember how I got to my pillow. The morning sun started to dance through the window. I stretched, yawned, and sniffed again. I caught the distant smell of Shirley. I jumped off my pillow to find her. I stopped at the closed door. Shirley's floral fragrance slipped under the door. I backed up and charged the door. It opened and I leapt up on the bed.

"What the . . .?" Grandpa yelled.

I put my nose in his face.

"Stop it." He pushed me away. "Get out of here."

I licked Shirley's ears. She screamed. I dived under the blankets.

"Go, get out!" Grandpa shouted.

Shirley started to laugh. "Oh, Harvey, he's a puppy."

"BEN, get your dog." Grandpa's voice thundered through the house. "BEN! Get in here."

I heard the rush of water in the water-room and quick footsteps. I perked my ears and stopped moving. I poked my head out from under the blankets and saw my dad standing in the doorway.

"Beau, OFF." My dad pointed to the floor.

My tail started to wag again. I love beginnings. Every time I go to sleep and wake up, it's a new beginning. Anything is possible. I jumped off the bed and danced around my dad's feet.

"Sorry about that. When he thinks it's time to get up, he's pretty persuasive." He reached down and held my head so my eyes could not look away. "Beau, you know you're not allowed on the beds." He looked back at Shirley and Grandpa. "How about some breakfast?"

Grandpa pulled the blankets over his head and groaned, "Too much wine last night."

"How about those Dutch pancakes I made last year?" my dad offered.

Grandpa sat up. "Really? Those puffy ones with apples, or was it pears?"

"I can do either. They're both in season," my dad answered.

"How about pears?" Grandpa smiled.

Shirley scowled at Grandpa and turned to my dad. "We don't need any special fuss."

"Hey," Grandpa interrupted, "Let him make pancakes if he wants to." Grandpa jumped out of bed. "Excuse me, I need to see a man about a horse." He quickly left the room.

I heard the door slam.

"EWWW!!" Grandpa shouted from the water-room. "WHO STUNK UP THE BATHROOM?"

My dad shook his head. "Classy." I followed him into the eating-room, and soon all the noises that meant food filled the room. Something started to sizzle. I moved directly underneath to wait for the flyaway drops.

Shirley walked into the room. "Nothing says good morning like the smell of bacon and coffee." She smiled at my dad.

"Help yourself to the coffee. I think it's done." My dad handed her a cup.

I ran to my empty food bowl and waited.

"Thanks." Shirley poured her cup and then sat down at the table. "That was such a nice dinner party last night."

"Your gumbo was a hit."

"You have such lovely friends." Shirley added.

My dad stirred something in a bowl. "By the way, what did you mean about giving Harvey a chance?"

"I know you can't take away the past, but you could try harder to make something new."

"I wouldn't know where to begin."

"Maybe you just need to spend more time looking on the bright side. As they say, turn your lemons into lemonade."

"Sorry, some lemons will always be lemons."

"Ben, your mother's horrible accident hurt your dad too."

"It's not really an accident when someone swallows two bottles of Valium. But, on some level, I admire her. She had courage to do the unthinkable."

Shirley frowned. "That's not courage."

Grandpa walked into the eating-room. "Got any aspirin? My head feels like it's going to explode."

I barked and ran to my food bowl. Maybe Grandpa would feed me.

"Just tell me where it is. I couldn't find it in the bathroom." Grandpa kissed Shirley. "Ben, your medicine cabinet looks like a pharmacy. You don't have a problem with prescription drugs, do you?"

My dad turned and faced Grandpa. "Why are you going through my cabinets?"

"Don't be so sensitive. I was just looking for the aspirin."

My dad walked out of the eating-room.

Shirley shook her head and scolded, "Harvey!"

Grandpa shrugged his shoulders and got a cup and sat down at the table. My dad returned and dropped a small bottle on the table. Shirley poked Grandpa with her elbow.

"Sorry . . . for being a grouch," Grandpa muttered. "I'll be better after this headache goes away."

My dad took a big breath. "Let's just eat."


ALL THE BAGS were by the door. My tail was moving fast. Bags meant that something was going to happen.

"Thank you, Ben, it was a wonderful weekend." Shirley wrapped her arms around my dad and kissed his forehead. "You've got to come to Scottsdale. Bring your friends. The desert is beautiful in the winter."

"I'll try. Thanks for all your help in the kitchen."

Grandpa held out his hand. "Good to see you." He shook my dad's hand and, with the other hand, patted my dad on his back.

"Bye, Harvey."

"Take care of yourself." Grandpa squeezed my dad's arm. "Don't get too skinny."

"Leave him alone, Harvey, he's probably on a diet." Shirley smiled.

There was a honk outside.

"I'm fine. Your cab's here." My dad opened the front door and blocked me from running out. "Have a good flight. Call me when you get in."

"We love you," Shirley said as she walked out.

Grandpa followed but stopped in front of my dad like he was going to say something, but then he turned and walked down the stairs, "Bye, Ben."

Grandpa and Shirley got into a waiting four-wheels, waved, and drove away. My dad slowly closed the door.

"We survived. Welcome to the family, Beau."

He walked with heavy feet down the hallway. I trotted behind him. He went into the sitting-room and sank into one of the soft chairs. I jumped into his lap. He sat for a long time staring at the wall, slowly petting me. I was starting to get sleepy. All of a sudden he jumped up.

"That's it," he said as I dropped to the floor.

He quickly walked to the eating-room. I followed. He opened a cabinet door and grabbed all the bottles that rattled and then walked to the water-room. I followed. He pulled open a drawer and took out more bottles.

"I'm done. No more."

One by one, he opened each bottle and emptied them into the water-chair. They made tiny splashes.

"I'd rather do nothing." My dad watched the floaters in the water and then started talking to them. "You make me sick, and having you around is like having an AIDS tattoo. I don't need you. I'll find another way." He pressed the water handle, and there was the rush of moving water.

He sat down on the floor and stared into the water-chair. I wiggled into his lap. He slowly ran his hand up and down my back. I curled into a ball. A couple sprinkles fell on my head. I looked up and saw water drops sliding down his face.

"This will be better." He looked down at me. "Sorry, kid, you don't get a vote," he said softly.

# Chapter 11

# Balls

Once I made it down the front steps, I stopped at the first patch of dirt I found. The gurgling inside my stomach bubbled up. I opened my mouth wide and out came a long blast. I stood still and waited. The gurgle started again. My insides rushed up, but this blast had less goo. I barely caught my breath before the next wave came. This time there was only yellow foam.

"Gross! Beau, what'd you eat?" My dad stood next to me with his nose scrunched.

The gurgling stopped. I smelled the stinky bile.

"LEAVE IT, don't eat it!" my dad shouted.

It smelled faintly familiar, but the rancid scent said "no." I backed up and walked away.

"I hope you got whatever nasty thing you ate out of your system." My dad followed me down the sidewalk. "We can go to the park, but you're not getting off the leash today."

When we made it to the park, for some reason the grass looked delicious. I choose the long, slender blades and started to munch.

"What are you doing?" My dad tried to pull me away.

I planted on all fours and continued to eat.

"Well, I guess it can't hurt you." My dad relaxed the leash.

The grass wasn't my usual thing. It was bitter and strange to eat. But I chomped, chewed, and swallowed. After several mouthfuls, we continued our walk. I kept my eyes open for more of the special grass. My nose wandered from smell to smell with little interest. I felt no need to pause and sniff. When we got home I wasn't ready to go inside. I knew I had more to do.

"Come on, Beau, I need to get ready for work." My dad pulled me into the house.

Inside, my dad headed to the eating-room. I followed but my tail wasn't moving. My dad made the usual morning noises and smells. I sat and watched. My tummy was silent and uncertain. My dad got my food bowl and filled it with the clanging patter of my food. I didn't move.

"Here's your breakfast, Beau."

I watched him put the bowl down. I didn't get up. There wasn't the racing of my heart or the drool that always sent me running toward the bowl.

"Come on, Beau, eat your breakfast."

I sat and looked at my dad instead of the bowl.

"Are you kidding me?" My dad's voice sounded worried. "You're going to say no to food?" He stared at me in silence. Then his voice changed to soft, "Little guy, what's wrong?"

My stomach made a rumble noise. I moaned and then ran to the back door.

"You have to go out again?" My dad shook his head and opened the back door. I barely made it down the stairs to the yard before I tossed up green, slimy syrup.

"You're really sick, poor thing. Guess we're going to the vet."

I wandered around the backyard and stopped when I found a few blades of green grass.

"No way." My dad hurried toward me. "You aren't eating any more of that."

He grabbed my collar and walked me inside. He sat down to eat his breakfast. I returned to the back door and sat.

"Give me a break, we just got in." My dad gave a big sigh, got up, and opened the back door. He stayed inside. The door closed behind me. My stomach heaved, but this time nothing came out.


"HEY JUDY," my dad said into the talking-machine. He sounded very tired.

"I'm OK but Beau's sick. He's been throwing up all morning."

"I called in sick and took him to the doctor."

"The vet's not sure. I think he ate something he shouldn't, but the vet did a physical exam and took an X-ray and didn't find anything. He said that sometimes it's hard to see or feel if there's a foreign object. Then he completely changed course and said that he thought Beau had pancreatitis. He gave him some meds."

"I used to think he was a good vet, but it feels like he's just guessing."

"I wish Beau could tell me. You should see him. It's so hard to see him like this."

My tummy was sore and empty, but I didn't want food. My dad had tried to feed me white food, but I said no.

"I'm supposed to watch him and bring him back if he doesn't get better."

"It's teacher in-service, so it's a good day to take off."

Nothing seemed familiar. I couldn't find the soft spot in my pillow. No matter where I moved, it felt wrong.

"Would you? I could use the company."

"Thanks. See you soon."

My dad put down the talking-machine and then quickly picked it up again.

"Hi, Anthony."

"No, I'm at home. I don't need you to walk Beau today."

"I didn't go to work. Beau's really sick."

"Yeah, I took him to the vet this morning."

"He wasn't very helpful, nothing definite. It's just wait and see."

"Thanks, but you don't need to. Judy's coming over."

"OK, sure, we'd love your company too."

My dad looked at me.

"You should see him Anthony. He looks so sad. Can you believe he walked away from steamed rice and chicken?"

"I know. Something's really wrong."

"Thanks."

"Bye."

I WHIMPERED. The day had disappeared, and the sitting-room glowed with flickering lights. My dad sat on the floor next to my pillow. Judy and Anthony sat next to him. My dad softly petted my head, but it didn't make me feel better. It was strange. My dad always filled my belly when I was hungry, walked me when I was full. He knew all the places to scratch, knew how to throw a ball so it bounced, knew when to tug my rope and when to let me shake it free. He always knew what to do.

"He looks so confused, poor baby," Judy said.

"If only he could talk," Anthony added.

My dad changed his petting and started to gently rub my ears. "There's nothing worse than being around someone who is really sick when there's nothing you can do to make them better."

"Especially if you love them." Judy nodded. "

I started to pant.

"I hate not knowing." My dad sighed.

"Have the meds made any difference?" Anthony asked.

"I don't think so." My dad carefully slid his hand down to my stomach. He looked at Anthony. "You didn't have to take tonight off from work."

"Are you kidding? Our baby is sick. Don't you think you should call the vet again?" Anthony voice rose.

"They closed at seven. I'd have to take him to the animal hospital." I stared at my dad as he talked. "If he's not better in the morning, I'll take him back to the vet."

"He looks like such a little boy." Judy shook her head. "Remember being sick as a kid? I hated being sick. My mom was weird around illness. She thought it was a weakness. She used to say, 'Just because you don't feel well, doesn't mean you have to act sick.' She thought that the best medicine was acting like you weren't sick."

Anthony's eyes opened wide. "Wow, that's harsh."

"She was especially tough on you," my dad added. "I think she didn't want you to be weak."

"Yeah, she wasn't big on weak." Judy continued, "She fought her cancer like a warrior. She never complained, never asked for help. She believed a positive attitude meant doing everything on her own."

My dad stopped petting for a moment. "I admired your mom. She was so strong and independent, but she did expect everyone to rise to her standards, especially you. My mom, on the other hand . . ."

I groaned. Although my dad's touch didn't make the pain go away, I wanted his hands to keep moving.

"Shhh, Beau, go to sleep." My dad's fingers resumed their journey up and down my back. He turned to Judy and then Anthony. "Life with my mom was a roller coaster."

"How was she when you were sick?" Anthony's hand joined my dad's in gentle circles on my belly.

"Hard to describe." My dad shrugged his shoulders. "She doted on me. There wasn't anything she wouldn't do for me when I was sick. But I always felt like she was keeping a tally sheet and eventually I would have to pay my debt."

I closed my mouth. My cheeks puffed and deflated with each breath.

Judy softly petted my forehead. "Sounds like love with lots of strings attached."

"Yeah, but the other side of her mothering was that she'd drink herself into a depression. Then she would ignore me; no more strings, no more mothering."

I sank deeper into my pillow.

My dad continued. "I remember when I had the chicken pox. I woke up with red spots everywhere. I was totally freaked out. When I showed my mom, she fussed over every red dot, held me while she read to me, and made me chicken soup. Unfortunately, by evening she was plastered and then I was invisible."

Anthony moved his hand in bigger circles. "My mom loved us most when we were sick. I think it took away all the confusion of motherhood. Her job was simply to nurse us. We loved it. She always set us up in the living room in front of the TV. She waited on us hand and foot and always made flan. To this day nothing says love like flan."

"Must have been nice." Judy sighed and rested her hand on my head.

"Well, she was Mrs. Cleaver when we were sick, but she became Mommy Dearest when we recovered. Guess no one escapes childhood unscathed." Anthony's hand continued to roam.

"That's why friends are better than family," Judy said. "It's less complicated when you need help."

"But it's hard to ask for help from anyone," my dad replied. "Look what it took for me to get help with my drinking."

"Things could have been different if you had gotten sober sooner," Anthony agreed.

My dad looked away. "Guess I had to crash first. That was quite the night. Once I sobered up enough to realize I was in the ER with alcohol poisoning, I didn't know what to do. I felt so depressed and alone. When the nurse asked whom to call, I made some bad joke about going to the Golden Gate Bridge, but she didn't find it funny. Instead I won a trip to San Francisco General Psych Ward."

Judy looked at Anthony. "That must have been a shock, to hear Ben's name during evening rounds."

"I knew he had an alcohol problem but HIV was a shock."

The touch and warmth of hands made my breathing slow and my eyes began to get heavy.

"I'm sorry," my dad said. "I was a mess."

"Still are." Judy rolled her eyes and smiled.

"But at least you're a sober mess," Anthony chimed in.

"What a ride! I drank because I didn't want to live, and I got sober because I didn't want to die, only to find out that I had HIV. Ain't life a kick in the pants?"

"Why did you stop going to AA?" Judy asked.

"I hate feeling dependent on anything, and I've been able to stay sober without the meetings. And I have mixed feelings about the higher-power stuff."

"Hmm," Judy said, "I guess we all have our messes. Look at what Beau has pulled together, three big messes."

Anthony's big hand rested on my head. "Looks like he's finally settling down," he said softly.

"Hopefully," my dad replied.

"Do you want us to spend the night?" Judy asked.

"That's OK. I think we'll be OK. I'll call you in the morning if I take him to the vet."

"Call either way," Anthony added.

"OK, I will."

Judy leaned down and kissed my head. "Get better, Beau."

Anthony patted my back. "Buddy-boy, you better be up for our walk tomorrow. I need my man magnet."

They both started to get up. I raised my head and then put it back down.

"I don't think he'll be walking you to the door tonight," my dad said as he stood up too.

They all walked to the front door. I heard their voices, the door open and then close.

My dad returned. "Let's go to bed, little man, and hope for a quiet night."

My dad left the light on low in our sleeping-room. He lay on his side and watched me for a long time, and then his breathing turned heavy and slow. His eyes were closed and his eyelids started to twitch. I couldn't sleep. My insides were full of strange activity. The constant rumble turned into a sharp pain. I let out a cry and my dad's eyes opened.

"Hey, are you OK?" he said, low and husky.

I stared back. The pain returned to a dull ache. His hand dropped down from his blankets and rested on my head.

"It'll soon be morning. Go to sleep, Beau."

I stared at him. His eyes slowly closed and once again his breathing slowed. His arm dangled above me.

My body was restless and I started to pant, faster and faster. Something moved deep inside of me. I couldn't do this all night. And then I felt it coming. I had no time to get out of the way. Up, up it came like an angry growl. It was a big chunk of my orange-and-blue ball covered in greasy slime. Finally, my insides became quiet.

It's horrible when something good turns into something bad. I really didn't mean to eat the ball. I love balls. It just happened.

I moved off my pillow to get away from the slimy mess. I found a nice spot on the hard floor. I curled up, exhausted, and sank deep into my sleep. Tomorrow I'd have to find another ball.

# Chapter 12

## Mine

The leash was clipped to my collar as we stood at the open front door. The talking-machine rang, and my dad slammed the door and ran back into the house. I raced after him with my leash trailing behind. As I turned the hallway corner, my leash got caught in the door and yanked me backward. My dad ran on without me.

"Hello."

"Oh, hi Anthony."

"We're just heading out to Duboce Park. I want to get out before the next rain."

"No, it's OK."

"Yeah, I saw it on the news. I don't believe it. Clinton wouldn't be that stupid. Paula Jones looks like an opportunist and Clinton has lots of enemies."

"Yes, I remember the Clarence Thomas hearings. Anita Hill was different."

"Time will tell."

"How are you?"

"We're good. Beau is completely back to his old self. I got new balls that are indestructible. He can't tear them up. And I'm good, actually, REALLY good," my dad said with excitement.

I pulled hard on the leash. My collar tightened around my neck. I whimpered and then barked. I wanted to be in the same room as the happy words.

"I'm feeling so much better. I'm taking a break from my meds. My stomach has really settled down. I've got more energy. I feel like I've got my life back."

"I don't know how long of a break. If this keeps up, who knows?"

"I know that you disagree, but my body agrees with me. You know I'm not alone. They call it a drug holiday."

"No, I haven't seen the doctor. I'm feeling good, why would I want to ruin a good thing? I'm doing supplements and eating well. There are some doctors who think the illnesses from HIV are actually some form of malnutrition."

"Just be happy for me. You know that usually I'm a glass-half-empty kind of guy, but my glass actually looks kinda full right now."

"Dinner sounds good. We could go to that French bistro in Glen Park. But, Anthony, don't plan on an intervention. I'm good, really."

"OK, next Wednesday. Can we call it our Christmas present to each other? Funds are a little tight after all of Beau's vet bills."

"OK."

"Bye."

I heard the click of the talking-machine. My dad came out of the eating-room and saw me.

"Oh, look at you! Did that mean ole leash get stuck in the door jamb?"

He let me go and I ran to find what was so exciting.

"Come on, Beau, let's go to the park."

My dad walked on without me. I did a quick stop and turn when I heard the door unlock and galloped to catch up. Everything outside looked washed. The sunshine made all the wetness sparkle. All the smells on the way to the park were dulled by water that dripped from leaves and the usual pee posts. The park's grass was squishy and cool, but the air was warm and bright.

When my dad released me from my leash, I scampered off to see who was at the park. There was only one dog, long and chunky with short legs. His belly hung low and sagged down to the grass. He stood silent and alert at his human's feet. I ran over to say hello, but he growled as I darted by.

"Hey, great day, huh?" My dad nodded to the human.

The human didn't answer.

"Come on, Beau," my dad mumbled as he moved toward the other side of the park. With some distance he added in a low voice, "Like father like son, but they won't steal our joy, right?"

I wandered around the park exploring the soggy smells. Out of the corner of my eye I saw a human and a hairy golden dog get out of their four-wheels and head toward my dad.

As they arrived the human smiled at my dad, "Morning,"

He was tall and thin. His cheeks were patchy red and his face was covered with red whiskers.

The sun bounced off the top of his shiny, pink hairless head. I remembered him from somewhere.

My dad smiled. "Morning. Finally some sunshine, huh?"

Red-whiskers smiled back. "It's pretty awesome."

"Nice to know someone appreciates it." My dad pointed to the yappy dog and his human. "The grump over there didn't even answer when I said good morning."

"It takes all kinds."

"I guess."

Red-whiskers looked harder at my dad. "Do I know you?" He cocked his head. "Oh, I know . . . Ben, right? You probably don't remember me, but I was the guy at the airport cargo counter when your puppy arrived." His voice had a familiar friendly bounce.

My dad turned. "Uhhhh?" He smiled. "Oh yeah, I remember . . . remind me of your name."

Goldie danced on her tiptoes, her long hair sashaying with every move. I ran over to sniff.

"It's Mike," he said with a bright toothy smile. I did a quick sprint and stopped, hoping Goldie would follow. She leaped and pulled hard on her leash. "And this is my girl, Farrah, who still loves to play." He unhooked the leash, and Farrah raced over to me and crouched in the "do you want to chase or be chased" position. "And this must be your puppy. He's gorgeous. What's his name?"

I ran around my dad's legs and Farrah ran after me, almost knocking him down.

"This is Beau and he likes to be chased."

Mike chuckled. "Does it run in the family?"

My dad laughed. "Maybe, I don't know. Things have been crazy, you know with a new puppy and all. I don't seem to have much time for anything else."

"I'm just teasing. Is this your neighborhood park?"

"Yeah, but we split our time between here, Buena Vista, and Corona Heights. It's nice to see you again. Where do you live?"

"The Sunset, but I was doing errands in the Castro so I decided to swing by this park. I'm glad I did."

Farrah and I took off and ran from one end of the park to the other. Every time we ran past the yappy dog, he gave us a shrill bark. We ended our loops around the park with a tumble and wrestle in front of my dad and Mike.

Mike laughed. "They're sure having fun."

"Yeah, we should plan a get-together sometime."

"That would be great. Farrah's always up for a play date."

"That'd be cool, but I mean WE should get together sometime," my dad smiled.

"Really? That'd be even better. When?" Mike paused and laughed. "Did that sound too eager?"

"How about dinner? Are you available tomorrow night? I'll cook."

"Wow, when you move, you really move. I'd love to. Can I bring anything?"

"No, just yourself." My dad handed Mike a piece of paper. "Here's my card, say about 7:00?"


"HEY, ANTHONY." My dad's voice was bright

and breathless.

"Still great," he said into the talking-machine.

"Guess what? I've got a date tomorrow night, a real date. I'm even cooking dinner."

"Do you remember the guy I told you about at Alaska Airlines when I picked up Beau?"

"Yeah, last spring."

"He gave me his number but I never called him. I just ran into him at the park and he recognized me. He's hot. He's a ginger with a great copper beard, green eyes, and a butt that just begs to be noticed. And he's really sweet."

"I don't know what got into me. I just decided to go for it. Next thing I knew I'd invited him to dinner and he said yes. Amazing, huh?"

"Don't over-analyze it, Dr. Freud."

"Honestly, I think it's because I lost my tether to the toilet."

"Thanks. I've got a good feeling about this guy. I'll give you the full report on Wednesday."

"Wish me luck."

"Bye."


THE DOORBELL chimed and I raced down the hallway. The multicolored rugs that my dad had carefully placed along the floor scattered in all directions. My dad followed, straightening them and muttering. When he arrived at the front door, he ran his hand through his hair one more time.

He turned to me. "Now, let's try and make a good impression."

When the door opened I raced outside. My dad tried to grab me. I jumped on Mike and hopped up and down. I ran back into the house and then out again. Mike started to laugh.

"Beau, get back here," my dad shouted.

Laughing and shouting don't usually go together, so I danced faster.

My dad grabbed my collar. "Sorry about that. We are still working on listening."

"It's OK. I remember those days with Farrah. That puppy energy overrides everything. He'll get it eventually," Mike reassured.

They hugged.

"Good to see you. Where's Farrah?" My dad looked out the front door.

"I didn't think you'd want your house turned into the Indy 500. And I thought she'd be too much of a distraction." Mike's eyes sparkled and he flashed a big smile.

"You could've brought her. Beau would've loved some help with distractions."

"Hopefully there'll be other chances." Mike bent down. "Hey, little guy, Farrah says hi."

I squirmed away from my dad's hold and put my nose in Mike's face. He rubbed me with both his hands and then flipped me over on my back and patted my belly.

"Oh, such a flirt, you like this, don't you?" Mike cooed.

I was right where I loved to be. Hands are amazing. They must be human's most prized possession. Hands make things happen. It must be why humans are in charge. When hands glide over me I know that I am in the center of the world. It's easy to get lost in the stroking. Sometimes I even lose track of who owns the hands. They feel like they're mine.

My dad and Mike sat on the floor.

"So, how do you like fatherhood?" Mike asked.

"I love it, but it's way more work than I ever imagined. He's like a toddler. He's got to be constantly watched. He gets into everything."

My dad stopped petting, so I rammed my head into his hand. His hand began to slide over my back again.

Mike laughed. "That sounds about right. How old is he?"

"Nine months."

"It will get easier but every dog is different. Farrah is three-years-old, and she still has lots of puppy in her. I thought Golden Retrievers were supposed to be mellow, but so far that's not Farrah."

"I think you're scaring me," my dad grimaced.

My dad stopped petting again, so I hopped off his lap and ran over to Mike. He immediately started to scratch my ears. "Something smells wonderful," he said as he inhaled.

"Thanks. It's lasagna," my dad replied.

"Yum. I can't cook to save my life. What a treat!" Mike smiled and stopped scratching.

I ran and got my new squishy, green ball and dropped it in Mike's lap.

Balls are an extension of human hands. When hands don't work, balls do. No matter where they roll, I can always find them. I always bring them back — they get re-touched, re-thrown, and then I find them again.

Mike picked up the ball and threw it down the hallway. I chased it down and trotted back.

"Dinner is almost ready. Let's head to the kitchen." My dad stood up.

"Great." Mike stretched and stood.

They walked away. The ball hung from my mouth. I sighed and dropped it. I ran toward savory smells in the eating-room and found my dad and Mike already sitting at the table. The lights were low, and several tiny fires flickered on the table.

"Nice place, Ben, very cozy. No Christmas tree?"

"I thought about it, but I wasn't sure Beau was ready for balls made of glass."

"You've got a point."

"Plus, it's always a little depressing taking it down."

"Really? I love the whole process, but that probably comes from a mother who has a storage shed with just Christmas stuff and she was never in a hurry to take anything down."

"Christmas was a little hit and miss in my family." My dad raised his eyebrows. "But that's a story for another time."

"I know the holidays can be complicated." Mike paused, "Mmmm, smells fantastic."

"Thanks. And you haven't even tasted it yet. I hope you'll never look at lasagna the same." My dad smiled and took Mike's plate and piled it with steaming food. The smells floated down to me and filled my nose with a saucy tang. I sat next to my dad's chair and stared.

"Wow, this looks wonderful." Mike's smile sparkled in the dim light. "You're incredible."

Mike leaned over and put his lips on my dad's lips. My dad took little nibbles on Mike's lips. Mike moaned and nibbled back. They looked like they were getting dizzy as they wobbled in their chairs.

Then they slowly broke away, breathing hard. They stared at each other with droopy eyes.

I whimpered.

"Wow, that was nice." My dad spoke low and slow.

Mike started to chuckle. "And I haven't even tried the lasagna yet. Can you imagine what I'll do if it's as good as you say?"

I barked.

My dad was sitting right in front of me. I could see him. I could smell him. But he was barely there.

"I think he's having a hard time sharing my attention," my dad said.

"Well, he's used to having you all to himself. It's hard to share." Mike's hand slid through my dad's hair. "I love your hair. Even when I had hair, it wasn't like this."

My dad smiled and his cheeks turned rosy. I jumped high into the air, and my body landed with a thump.

Mike laughed, "I think he's having a meltdown."

"Excuse me for a minute." My dad pushed away from the table and stood up. "Beau, it's time to chill out on your bed."

I danced. My dad was back.

My dad pointed. "Go to bed."

I ran and got my ball.

"No." My dad's voice was firm. He pointed to my pillow again. "Down."

I walked over to my pillow and lay down. I watched my ball, waiting for him to pick it up.

"Stay!" my dad said in his deep voice.

He turned and started to walk back to the table. I got up and followed. I heard Mike laugh.

My dad spun around and pointed. "Beau, go back to your bed."

I slowly walked back.

"Good boy." My dad sounded friendlier. "Down . . . stay."

I lay down.

"Good boy, that's a good boy." My dad went over to the counter and came back with a treat. I gobbled it up.

"Now stay." My dad started to walk away and then turned around. "Stay!"

I took a deep breath and slumped into my pillow. I buried my head under my paws. I drifted off to sleep with the chatter of talking and the clink and clank of humans eating.

When I woke up the house was dark except for the little fires glimmering on the table. Mike and my dad were no longer eating. They were talking softly. Their chairs were close together and they held hands.

I jumped up.

"Looks like someone woke up," Mike chuckled.

"And I think he wants to join the party," my dad laughed.

"Hi, little guy, did you have a good nap?" My dad reached down and rubbed my back.

I sat down and leaned into my dad's leg, as his hand ran down my back to my belly.

"Well, Ben, I should be going. It's late. I had a wonderful time. Thank you."

"Thanks for coming over. I hope we can do this again." My dad pulled his hand away from my back.

"Me too." Mike stood up. He moved over to my dad and sat down, straddling his lap. "I hope there's more."

They faced each other and their lips locked together, making slurping sounds. Their hands petted and roamed. Once again I had lost my human hands. I tried to jump up into their laps but fell backward. My dad and Mike started to giggle.

"He really does want to be included." Mike picked me up and put me in the middle of their hug.

"Yeah, he's the jealous type," my dad said.

I squirmed, sniffing and licking.

"Don't worry, little guy." Mike's fingers scratched my head. "There's room for you." He leaned into my dad and their lips connected again.

# Chapter 13

## Three-Legs

Farrah and I sat in the eating-room, eyes focused on the floor. Mike was chopping on the counter. Farrah and I both knew that chopping meant food chunks would be jumping to the floor. Suddenly, Farrah leaped up and ran toward Mike's feet. I followed but was too slow. Farrah gobbled up the jumper. We continued our watch.

"How much should I chop these onions?"

"Pretty fine," my dad answered.

Mike stopped chopping. "I'm excited to meet Anthony and Judy."

"I've held them off for as long as I can. They can't wait to meet you, I mean, interview you, either. I don't know whether they're looking out for me or wanting to warn you. I hope you're ready."

"I'll do my best. Are you ready for the onions?"

"Yeah, put them in the pan."

Splatter noises filled the room. Farrah sat unaware. I knew that splatter meant rain, tasty rain, and quickly licked up the tiny drops that fell to the floor. The first drizzle was gone by the time Farrah caught on.

"I love risotto, but I wouldn't ever think of trying to make it." Mike moved over to my dad and kissed his neck.

"Back to your post. Risotto gets very angry if she's ignored." My dad pushed Mike away and patted his butt as Mike returned to the sizzling pan. "Sauté them until they're translucent. Don't let them brown."

"I love it when you're bossy."

"Shut up and stir." My dad was smiling his friendly, silly smile.

The doorbell rang. I tore off toward the front door, Farrah on my heels. We both were barking. I came to a sliding stop. Farrah slid into me, and we slammed into the door together with a bang.

"Wow." There was laughter on the other side of the door.

My dad arrived at the door and pushed Farrah and me out of the way. He opened the door and we ran around him.

"Beau, Farrah, get back." My dad tried to block our escape.

Judy was standing at the door, shaking her head.

"Hi, Judy." My dad hugged her as she walked into the house.

Anthony was outside. "Hi Beau, who's your girlfriend?" He squatted down and petted us.

My dad watched from the door. "This is Farrah, Mike's dog."

Anthony looked around and whispered, "Where is he?"

My dad pointed to the eating-room.

"Oh Judy, look, it's a blended family." Anthony's hands made their way down our backs.

"Come here, Beau," Judy called to me. "Come give some lovin' to your Auntie."

I ran over to Judy and Farrah followed. When Judy bent down I put my nose in one ear, and Farrah put her nose in the other. Judy laughed, "Hey, they both do the ear thing."

Anthony hugged my dad. "I can't wait to meet this man."

My dad took Anthony's hand and reached down for Judy's hand. "Well, let's get this over with."

Farrah and I ran between their legs and raced ahead. We got to the eating-room first. Mike was standing tall and smiling.

My dad walked into the eating-room. "Judy and Anthony, this is Mike. Mike, this is Judy and Anthony." My dad turned around and started to lead Judy and Anthony out of the room. "That was fun, thanks for coming, bye."

"I don't think so." Judy broke free and headed back toward Mike.

Mike stepped forward with his hand outstretched. "Hi, Judy."

"Nice to meet you," Judy said as she shook Mike's hand.

"Hi, Anthony." Mike reached for Anthony's hand.

Anthony ignored the hand and pulled Mike into a hug. "It's great to meet you." Anthony stepped back and looked at Mike. "Well done, Ben."

My dad and Mike's faces started to change color.

"Anthony, you're embarrassing them. Nice job!" Judy pinched my dad's cheek. "This is going to be fun."

"You two better behave. Dinner could be optional." My dad sounded mad but looked happy.

"We're harmless, Mike. Seriously, it's really nice to meet you. Anyone who can make Ben happy makes us happy, cuz lord knows Ben ain't easy." Judy handed my dad a bottle. "Here's the wine."

"Was he?" Anthony pointed to my dad. "Easy, that is?" Anthony chuckled.

My dad pointed his finger at Anthony. "Ignore him, he's crazy." My dad got some glasses out of the cabinet. "Let me lace his glass with his lithium. He obviously didn't take his meds."

"Speaking of easy, what do you think about President Clinton and Monika Lewinsky?" Anthony's eyes widened.

"Politics and sex is the oldest story in Washington," my dad answered.

"Wouldn't it be terrible if he gets caught in a lie." Anthony added.

"Terrible to get caught, or terrible to lie?" Judy asked but then shook her head. "Never mind, no politics tonight. I'm sick of all of it. Ben, do you need any help with dinner?"

"Good call, Judy. Actually, what I really need is someone to take Beau for a walk." My dad looked at Judy with big eyes. "Would you?"

"Farrah and I will go with you," Mike offered.

"Great, then I can get some private time." Judy smiled at Ben.

"Suddenly I'm not so sure this is a good idea." My dad wrinkled his forehead. "Only tell him the good stuff."

"Let's go, kids." Judy snapped my leash on my collar. Mike did the same to Farrah. We all walked down the hallway, but I kept looking back at my dad.

"Oh go ahead, Beau, don't be such a daddy's boy," my dad waved his hand at me.

Mike, Judy, and Farrah walked out the front door and I followed. The night was colored with a yellow glow. The air was crisp.

"What a gorgeous moon." Judy looked up at the sky.

"I love clear winter night in San Francisco." Mike breathed in deeply. "It feels so alive."

"Hmm," Judy looked at Mike and smiled.

We headed out into the not-yet-dark night. Farrah and I hurried to smell the hot spots. Shadows pretended to be what they were not, but my nose told the truth.

"So, Mike, you work for Alaska Airlines?"

"Yeah, in their cargo department. I don't deal with passengers, just shipping."

"And that's how you first met Ben?"

Farrah and I stopped to sniff a tree trunk. Mike and Judy stopped too. The sour scent of an older dog ran down the tree and puddled on the ground. Farrah and I studied the smell. Something was strange.

"Yup, it was the day he got baby Beau. I still remember that starry look in Ben's eyes — maybe more like a deer in the headlights. He was adorable . . . vulnerable."

"Have you told him that?"

"Come to think of it, I don't think I have."

"Probably just as well. He thinks he's tough." Judy tugged my leash. "Come on, Beau, let's go."

My nose was pulled away from the scent, and the leash grew tight. I strained my head to get another sniff but Judy was moving, taking me with her.

Mike followed with Farrah. He turned to Judy. "If this is too personal, tell me, but you have a really unique relationship with Ben. How does it work?"

Judy made a loud noise that sounded like something between a laugh and a snort. "Honey, we'd have to walk a long time to excavate that one. The truth is, I don't really know. We have so much history, ugly *and* beautiful. I don't think either one of us can walk away. I hope this doesn't scare you, but I still consider him my husband. Obviously, we don't have sex, don't play house, but there is no one in the world that I love more. It's beautifully imperfect. Twisted, I know."

"I don't know. I think there are many forms of love."

Judy nodded. "I gave up on the Hollywood ending a long time ago."

Their voices stopped, and the night became quiet except for the thump of human feet and the click of paws. Shadows danced in front of us, and smells called out their names. Ahead of us a dim form slowly began to take shape. It moved with a drag, drop, and hop. Judy and Mike stared.

"Oh, how sad," Judy mumbled.

When we got close enough, the shadow became fur and flesh. I cocked my head and recognized Three-legs. His hair was matted in clumps surrounded by bald spots. He didn't turn as I approached. His nose pointed toward the sky, and he sniffed. When our noses bumped, he jumped.

"He's almost blind, and I don't think he smells much anymore either." Three-legs' human was gray-haired and stooped. He leaned on his own skinny third leg.

"What's his name?" Judy asked.

"Chester," the man replied.

Three-legs was breathing hard. He smelled like something that had spent too much time in the sun. He moaned.

"Hey, Chester, how's it goin'?" Mike patted Three-legs's head.

Judy sighed. "He looks brave."

"He is, but he doesn't know how to quit. The vet gave him one month, six months ago. Cancer. He lost his leg but he keeps on going."

Three-legs whined and pushed his head against Mike's hand.

"That must be so hard, for both of you," Judy said.

The man nodded his head and looked away. He gently tugged the leash. "Come on, Chester, let's go home."

Three-legs and the man shuffled down the sidewalk, no good-bye sniff.

"Good luck," Judy called after them.

They slowly crossed the street to the other side. We all watched.

"I can't imagine. I don't know if I could do it," Mike said softly.

"I guess it's not a choice," Judy replied. "You just deal with what you're given."

"I guess so. It's probably a good thing that we can't see what's in the future."

"Isn't that the beauty of a dog," Judy smiled. "They are totally about the present. They forget most of their past and don't look too far in the future. Maybe I can be a dog in the next life. I have to work really hard at being present. I've got a bad habit of always trying to see what's coming." Judy looked at her wrist. "We better hurry up. I'm sure you've already discovered that Ben can get bitchy about his food."

"Yeah, he does take his food seriously, and I didn't finish my risotto lesson, oh well. Don't tell Ben, but I'm not really interested in learning. I just like the company."

Judy and Mike laughed.


"PERFECT TIMING." My dad kissed Mike and then Judy. "Thanks for taking the dogs out. Now sit down. Let's eat."

Farrah and I ran to see if there had been any jumpers since we were away.

"How was it?" Anthony sat at the table and had a glass in his hand. "Any good gossip?"

"It's such a beautiful night. The moon is incredible." Mike sat down next to Anthony.

"Attaboy. Deflect, detour, and don't answer any questions." My dad carried two bowls to the table and sat down.

Judy sat next to my dad and across from Anthony and Mike. "We had a nice time." Judy nodded toward Mike. "Ben, he's lovely."

"Great, now that we have that out of the way, let's eat." My dad passed one of the bowls to Judy. "It's arugula with Asian pears and gorgonzola."

"Mmmm," Judy moaned.

"When do I get my turn with him?" Anthony put his arm around Mike. "We'll talk later."

Judy put some food on her plate and passed the bowl to Anthony. "On our walk we saw an old dog with an amputated leg. It was so sad."

Farrah and I weaved in and out of the human-and-table legs looking for fallen treats.

"That was Ernie and Chester." My dad added, "They're something, aren't they?"

Anthony took the bowl. "The other day I saw a dog without both back legs. He had some kind of cart with wheels attached so he could walk. It was amazing." Anthony put food on his plate and handed the bowl to Mike.

"I don't know, when I see dogs like that . . . it just seems cruel." Mike held the bowl in his hands.

"How so?" Anthony took a bite of food.

"Like it's for the owner, prolonging the dog's life at any cost. I can't imagine Farrah being unable to do the things she loves to do just so I can have more time. It just seems . . ."

Judy cut in, "I think dogs get something out of their relationships, too. Don't you think they appreciate the extra time?"

"Yeah, maybe, but what good is time if a dog can't do what they love?" Mike reached down to caress Farrah's head. "When Farrah's swimming or retrieving or chasing, you can tell she's not just doing but being whom she is meant to be."

Judy swallowed and got ready to scoop up more food. "What about when you scratch her ears or rub her belly? Extra time would give her more of those things."

My dad drank from his glass. "It's a hard decision either way. Some days I think Ernie and Chester are role models, and other days I think it looks like torture."

Judy shook her head. "I can't imagine making that decision. Maybe that's why I don't have pets."

Anthony picked up the bottle and poured more into his glass. "Farrah and Beau, don't listen to any of this."

"Oh, these two are going to be with us for a long time, right, kids?" My dad patted his lap.

Farrah and I raced over to him and put our front paws in his lap. We sniffed him and then looked at each other, wondering where he had hidden the treat.

MY DAD WAS in his bed and I was in mine. He had tossed and turned in his bed and finally had picked up the talking-machine.

"Hi Judy, I hope this isn't too late."

"Mike had to go home. He has an early shift tomorrow."

"It was a really nice evening. Nobody had to be ejected from the party." My dad chuckled.

"I haven't fully thanked you."

"For moving past my HIV news, or at least it feels like you let something go."

"Well, thanks. It means a lot to me."

"Yeah, I did have something to ask you. I think you know me better than anyone. It's a little strange, but I would like your perspective on something."

"Do you think I'm capable of being happy?"

"Well, the other day I was reading something about learned helplessness. They did these horrible experiments with dogs where they gave them shocks and didn't provide any way for them to escape. Eventually, the dogs just gave up. You don't think I'm like those dogs, do you?"

"I feel really happy right now, and it really scares me."

"I think I'm always afraid that I'm going to open a door and find a dead body."

"Yeah, I know it's really a long time ago, but I've always known it's not just about Mom's suicide. As a kid I always felt like something bad was going to happen, and no one talked about it. My mother's love was combustible. It makes it hard to trust happiness."

My dad listened a long time and then said, "Your meditation is paying off. You sound so wise."

"Guess that's why they call it a practice."

"I know relationships are hard work. I hope that I am up for it."

"Thanks, Judy. It helps to talk about it. It makes it less scary."

"Is it weird giving me relationship advice? I'd be happy to return the favor."

"You never know what's around the corner. I certainly didn't see Mike coming."

"I'll let you go to sleep. Thanks again."

"Good night."

# Chapter 14

## You and Me

Farrah and I snuggled together in the back of Mike's extra-big four-wheels. The back seat folded down into a giant bed. Farrah lay on her side, blonde hair flowing from her belly and her long bushy tail at times swishing across our bed. I curled up next to her outstretched legs. There's nothing quite like lying next to one of your own kind, four-legged and hairy. The excitement of my first trip with Farrah turned drowsy as the hum of rolling wheels and the chatter of my dad and Mike made my breathing turn slow and heavy. Farrah shifted and settled into our cuddle.

Mike glanced at my dad. "You're going to love the cabin." One of Mike's hands held onto four-wheels, and the other rested on my dad's knee. "It's next to a little lake and is surrounded by a grove of red fir. They had snow a couple of days ago so it should be beautiful. President's Day weekend is always great up there."

My dad smiled as he looked at Mike. "I can't wait. I love the snow but never get up to the mountains."

Mike's hand petted my dad's thigh. "My family has been going to the Sierras for years. My dad liked getting out of the city. He bought this cabin in the '50s. It has some of my best childhood memories."

"Do you only go in the winter?"

"No, I love it up there anytime of the year. The drive still makes me feel like a kid. My sisters and I used to fall asleep the minute we left the city, but we always woke around Auburn when the car started to climb into the foothills. There's just something about the mountains. Where did your family vacation?"

My dad made a short snort. "We weren't really the vacationing type."

My dad ripped open a bag and offered it to Mike. Spicy, pungent smells drifted to the back seat. I got up and poked my nose in Mike's ear.

Mike giggled. "Hey, stop that, no kissing while I'm driving."

My dad pushed me back. "Don't be fooled, he just wants some Doritos. Beau, get back there. This isn't for you. Go back to sleep."

I plopped back down next to Farrah. I couldn't believe she slept through the smelly tease.

My dad continued talking, crunching between words. "The only trip we ever took together was when I was ten. We drove cross-country from Arizona to Niagara Falls for my aunt's wedding. It wasn't much fun."

"What happened?"

"Well, we were all completely out of our comfort zone."

"What do you mean?"

"My father and mother did best when they had lots of space. They mostly avoided close quarters. We hardly ever all ate together or did much of anything as a complete family. Maybe we were afraid of what might come out if we were forced to be close. I spent a lot of time with my mom or alone in my bedroom with my art supplies. My dad used to camp out in front of the TV and watch sports. And when my mom got tired of me, well, she had her martinis."

"Sounds lonely."

"But it kind of worked — at least it mostly kept the peace. So family vacation was a radical idea. We were sequestered together in our powder blue Pontiac sedan for days, although I did love that car. My mom and dad bickered about most everything, but even worse was the silence. I can still see my mom staring out the window, still and stiff. I fantasized about getting left behind when we stopped for gas. But I guess the fear of doing something is always worse than the dread of staying put. It was that summer that I discovered public bathrooms. I was amazed by the stuff on the walls. Do you remember that moment when you realized that there were people like you? Even though those gas station and rest-stop bathrooms were seedy and dirty, it was amazing to know I wasn't the only one, not that I had any actual encounters. That summer I discovered masturbation, the great escape." My dad looked out the window. "In retrospect, I'm sure my mom had a mental illness. My dad didn't know how to help her. I tried hard but what can a kid do?"

"Wow."

"Yeah, welcome to my childhood. Yours sounds a bit happier."

Farrah twitched and whimpered in her sleep.

Mike shrugged his shoulders. "I did have a good childhood. However, adolescence was another story."

"How's that?"

"My parents didn't know what to do with us when we hit puberty. They were good Catholics. I have five sisters, so I'm sure sexuality was scary for my parents. Initially, I was the least of their worries, that is, until my dad walked in on me and Neil."

"Neil? Who's Neil?" My dad pinched Mike and chuckled. "So you had a childhood sweetheart! I'm jealous."

"Hardly. Neil was just the neighbor kid who liked to show everyone his penis. My dad caught us in the bathroom."

"Oh no."

Mike continued, "It's kinda funny now, but at the time I was mortified. My dad opened the bathroom door and there we were. He didn't scold or yell—just quietly closed the door. He never said anything about what he saw. But suddenly there were fewer goodnight kisses from my dad, we stopped rough-housing, and he started to really push me into sports. He must have told my mom because she started to always ask about girlfriends. Times were different then. We didn't really have any out role models. I don't think my parents had any idea what they were supposed to do." Mike paused then asked, "Did things get better in your family?"

"Some better, some not. I guess my stepmom tries hard, but she gets on my nerves. And my dad and I only know how to avoid or argue. My mom died when I was twelve."

"I'm sorry. Was it unexpected?"

My dad was quiet before he answered. "You could say that. She killed herself."

"Oh my God, that's horrible. I'm sorry. We don't have to talk about it if you don't want to."

"It's OK. It was twenty-two years ago. She medicated herself with booze and God — or I should say, Pastor Clayton's version of God, which only made things worse."

"What do you mean?"

"We used to go to a conservative church in Phoenix. Pastor Clayton took a special interest in our family. I think he was attracted to lost causes — the bigger the sinner, the more valuable the prize for saving them. My dad wouldn't have anything to do with church, but Pastor Clayton had lots of prayer sessions with my mom. I'm sure he didn't believe in mental illness or the disease of alcoholism. Every problem was a result of sin, and the solution was always prayer. My mom tried hard, but she just got better at hiding. Pastor Clayton spent a lot of time with me, too, and I was grateful for the attention. I got better at being good. He used to take me with him when he did door-to-door evangelism. I think I was the cute mascot that got people to open their doors. When my mom died I turned to Pastor Clayton for help. At some point I told him that I thought I liked boys. He convened the church elders, who read every passage in the Bible that talked about homosexuality, and then prayed over me, asking God to save me from my evil desires. I never went back, but I married Judy when I was twenty-one."

Mike sighed. "The Church has hurt a lot of people. It's amazing how much of the Bible they leave out when they get on their holy high horse."

"I do wonder if things would have been different if my mom had gotten treatment instead of preaching. Have things gotten any better with your parents?"

"Some. They've relaxed a bit, and I think they're relieved that I'm not a lecherous man in a trench coat." Mike smiled. "Plus, compared to my sisters' drama, my life is charmed."

My dad stared out the window. "I always felt like I was part of a mistake, like my family was traveling down a road based on a wrong turn. Maybe that's why my dad is so happy now. When my mom died he was set free. It took him awhile but eventually he remarried and got another chance. He was able to move on." My dad shook his head.

"Why can't you move on?"

My dad smiled. "I'm working on it."

I moved closer to Farrah. The heat of her stomach warmed my back. There is nothing like drifting off to sleep when you have company. It's not just that it's warm but it reminds me of a dream, snuggled with Mama, breathing in soft moans.


FARRAH AND I raised our heads at the same time. The smooth whirl of four-wheels became bumpy and gritty.

"Hey, kids, we're almost there." Mike called out.

Outside the window there were big trees with broad green branches holding mounds of white. Farrah and I put our noses close to the window. Our panting breaths bounced off the window and turned the window steamy.

My dad rubbed his hand across the window. "It's beautiful."

"Yep, it's something, isn't it? Hey look, someone shoveled a spot for skating." Mike pointed out the window. "Have you ever ice-skated?"

"Never, but I'm good at making a fool of myself."

"I'll teach you—how to skate, that is." Mike winked at my dad.

Farrah and I moved from window to window. Farrah was even more excited than me. She started to whine.

"Easy, girl, hold on." Mike nodded toward Farrah. "She loves it here. This place is dog paradise."

Four-wheels slowed and then stopped. Farrah jumped into the front seat and sat on Mike's lap.

Mike opened the door. "Off you go."

Farrah jumped out, and I somersaulted into Mike's lap and then rolled out the door. The ground was hard and cold. Snowflakes danced with each wind puff. It made my feet feel light and my nose dizzy with smells. Farrah chased the falling snow. I was right on her heels. She rolled in the white powder, and I jumped on top of her. Mike and my dad followed, dressed in puffy coats and hats. They headed toward the glassy lake.

"Let's check the ice," Mike said through steam coming from his mouth.

Once we got to the lake, Mike and my dad moved carefully, feet sliding instead of walking. I sat with Farrah at the edge of the lake and watched.

"I think I've got it," my dad said, as his feet took longer glides. All of a sudden his feet slid out from under him, and he grabbed for Mike. "Ahhhh, shit," my dad yelled. He caught Mike's arm and they both landed with a thud. After a brief silence, they both started to laugh, arms and legs entangled. I raced onto the ice and heard Farrah barking from the shore. I slid past my dad and Mike. My nails scratched and scraped as I tried to stop, but my feet pulled one way and then jerked another. I landed hard on my butt. When I tried to get up, my feet would not stay where I put them.

"Come on, Beau, you can do it." Mike called between snorts of laughter. I inched my way over, and Mike pulled me into the human pile. Steam and laughter, licks and wags, we rolled together on the cold, hard lake.

"Guess you both are going to need skating lessons," Mike chuckled, as he hugged my dad and me. I wiggled to get free and join Farrah on the frozen ground.

"So do you want to see the cabin?" Mike slowly stood up and offered his hand to my dad.

Farrah ran toward the house and I followed. When the door opened, Farrah and I pushed our way past Mike. The front room was as tall as a tree. A huge window looked out on the frozen lake, and one of the walls was covered with gray and brown stones. I ran after Farrah as she took off through the house.

"Brrrr, it's cold in here. I'll get a fire going." Mike started to pile up chunks of wood in the stone wall. "Ben, check out the kitchen."

"OK, I'll put the food away." My dad walked into the eating-room. "Wow, looks great."

The eating-room was separated from the tall room by a long counter. The food smells on the floor were old and faint. We ran up some steep stairs and found the sleeping-rooms. The biggest one overlooked the tall room below. I looked through the railing at Mike and my dad below. I smelled smoke and saw sparks jumping in the stone wall. Farrah grabbed one of my ears and play-growled. I put my head on the ground and slid it under Farrah, nipping at her ankles. She pinned me to the floor. I squirmed away and tore off down the stairs. Farrah chased me around the house and up and down the stairs. The house began to warm. We played until our tongues were hanging from our mouths. Farrah found the water bowl, and we drank long and hard. Suddenly I realized that the house was very quiet.

I ran up the stairs to the sleeping-room. My dad and Mike were standing in their skins. Mike was smooth and white with rust-colored dots. My dad was pink and hairy. Their arms were wrapped around each other and their clothes were scattered about. Farrah circled them once and then plopped down on Mike's fluffy coat. I sniffed their bare legs. They were warm and moist. I followed a musky scent up the backside of Mike's leg and stopped at his fragrant spot.

"Hey, Beau, stop that!" My dad pushed my head away from Mike's butt.

Mike chuckled and turned toward me. "Sorry, buddy, some things are off limits, even for you."

Mike was a strange sight. The tail-that-doesn't-wag between his legs wasn't hanging. It reached beyond a patch of curly red hair toward the sky. I glanced over at my dad, and his tail-that-doesn't-wag was also standing up. I moved over to my dad and raised my nose so I could sniff.

"HEY, STOP IT." My dad yelled and covered himself with his hands.

Mike laughed louder.

My dad smiled but his voice was stern. "Beau, go lay down." My dad pointed toward Farrah. "Go take a nap with your girlfriend."

He pulled my pillow out of one of his bags. He put it down next to Farrah.

"Here's your bed, now lay down."

I trotted over and flopped down. My dad bent down and patted my head.

"Good boy. Now, let your dad have some private time." His tail-that-doesn't-wag was no longer stretching. It was looking at the floor.

Mike climbed into the bed and called to my dad, "Get in here, this bed is cold."

My dad rummaged through one of his bags and took out a bottle and several small packets. He held them up and smiled.

Mike sat up and grinned. "Remember life before condoms . . . it was so much fun . . . maybe we could . . . we're both clean, right?"

My dad stood still. He looked scared. "I've got to go to the bathroom." My dad walked into the water-room and closed the door.

"Hurry up," Mike shouted. "It's lonely in this big bed."

Farrah put her head on my pillow. She smelled wet and musky from the melted snow. She closed her eyes and started her sleepy breathing. I closed my eyes too. I woke up when I heard the water-room door open.

"Is everything OK?" Mike asked carefully. "You were in there a long time."

"Yeah." My dad got into the bed.

They rolled together under the blankets, groaning and moaning. They tumbled this way and that. Mike ended up under my dad, breathing hard.

"Mmmm," Mike moaned.

Then slowly my dad rolled off of Mike and lay quietly next to him.

"Sorry." My dad stared at the ceiling.

"It's OK, it happens to the best of us." Mike stroked my dad's hair. "Really, it's OK." Mike smiled and slid his hand under the blankets. "I have confidence in your Mr. Man."

"I think we should use condoms," my dad said softly.

"That's cool. I just thought that maybe . . . you know. But don't get me wrong. It's been great these last few months, no complaints. Really!"

"OK." My dad pulled the blankets up to his chin.

Mike continued, "I just thought that maybe we could mix it up a bit."

My dad was quiet.

"I mean if you wanted to . . . but we don't have to." Mike ran his hands through my dad's hair.

"Let's use condoms." My dad sounded far away.

"No problem." Mike pulled my dad on top of him.

My dad looked down at Mike. "Would it be OK if we just cuddled?"

"OK." Mike sounded sad.

They rolled onto their sides and scooted close together.

Mike sighed. "We've got lots of time, right?"

# Chapter 15

## Dogs that Bite

After many grey and rainy days, things were starting to change. Without warning the days were getting longer. The muddy puddles and squishy grass were starting to dry up. The damp, chilly air that had been sneaking into our house was replaced with warmer air that smelled fresh and new. Anthony and my dad sat at the eating-room table. I wanted to be outside.

"Your uncle sounds like an ass. So he just called out of the blue?" Anthony picked up his cup and took a careful sip.

"Yeah, I haven't seen or talked to my uncle in years. He's my mom's brother." My dad stirred his cup and took a drink.

I moved over and sat on Anthony's feet.

"So why did he call?" Anthony reached down and patted my head.

"He said he was just thinking about me. Actually I think he said that he was worried about me, worried about my relationship to God."

I leaned into Anthony's leg. I wanted more than a pat.

"Oh, so it was just a social call to let you know that hell is getting hotter." Anthony rolled his eyes.

"Not quite. He called to tell me about that Christian group, Exodus, the one that claims to cure homosexuality. He was all excited and told me that there's hope."

"Hope for what? I'm sure he thinks it's a choice. It just pisses me off. Heterosexuals certainly don't think that their sexuality is a choice. I wonder if your uncle would like to talk to you about his sexuality choice. I'm sure it was a struggle for him to choose heterosexuality." Anthony took one of my ears into his hand and scratched.

"He's not gay." My dad frowned.

"Exactly my point. No one chooses his or her sexuality. Can I hear an Amen?" Anthony picked up one of my paws and raised it in the air. "Amen," he said in a squeaky voice.

"It's not funny." My dad sounded hurt. "He got to me."

Anthony sat up. "Seriously?"

Anthony wasn't making any signs of moving toward the door, so I went over to my dad and put my head in his lap. I exhaled loudly but my dad continued talking. "I guess it brought back some of my childhood tapes."

"How does he know you're gay?"

"You know families. When I got divorced it was just too titillating for my cousins to keep my sexuality quiet. They told my uncle." My dad put his hand on my head and let it just sit there. "Maybe I'm being paranoid, but I had this feeling that he knew I had HIV."

"He probably assumes that everyone who's gay has AIDS. But, Ben, really? If he did know, who cares? He's nobody."

"You've never wondered if it's God's curse?"

"Ben, I hope you're joking."

"Well, kinda, but what if this disease is some kind of communication from God?"

"Where's this coming from? You know homosexuality doesn't cause AIDS, HIV does. You want a message from God? Here's one. Jesus hung out with lepers, the diseased and social outcasts of his day. It was the AIDS epidemic of his time. He responded with compassion and kindness, not judgment. His judgment was saved for those who judged."

"But don't you ever wonder, just maybe?"

"Why are you going here? Who are you and what have you done with my Ben? I thought you let go of your Christian guilt."

I nudged my dad's leg. He looked down at me and started to rub my head.

Anthony continued, "Your uncle and those like him operate from fear. It's used to control and scare people into compliance. Those who use fear in the name of God are just trying to use the trump card to make people look and behave like them. The fact that you have a life-threatening illness makes you more susceptible to their manipulation, but it doesn't make them right. And just for the record, the next time your uncle calls let me talk to him. I'll singe his ear hair with some Latin fire!"

I ran and got my ball and dropped it next to Anthony. He picked it up. "Now, here's someone who never doubts his desires. Beau, you wanna go to the park?" I cocked my ears and raised my eyelashes up and down.

My dad stood up. "Good idea. Can you believe Beau's almost a year old?"

"How can that be?" Anthony picked me up and held me close to his face. "Is it true, old man?" I licked his nose.

"He'll be one next month. He was born April 13 and I got him in June."

"That's amazing. Where did the year go? Let's get you outside, big boy." Anthony snapped on my leash and we headed toward the door.

The air was mild. Tender green shoots were popping up in the soft mud, and bare trees were sprouting little buds and flowers from their long, bony branches. The birds, many which had lost their voices in the rainy, dark days, flittered with excited chirps and tweets. My tail answered the happy call. I love when the outside feels the same as my insides.

Anthony walked next to my dad and nudged him with his elbow. "So, I guess you're going to make me ask."

"Ask about what?" my dad said with a shrug.

Anthony stopped walking and put his hand on his hip. "Your weekend with Mike, you fool."

"That was last month."

"Well I've been trying not to pry, but enough is enough. How was it?"

"It was nice."

"NICE! Are you kidding me? Come on, stop teasing me. Give me the dish."

"Well, it was nice. The cabin was beautiful, set in the middle of a forest, next to a lake, big A-frame with lots of windows, great fireplace. It was really cozy."

"I feel like I'm talking to my mother. What about MIKE?"

"He's good, a sweetheart. We had a good time."

"Why do I hear a 'but' in there somewhere?"

My dad stopped to pick a pink and white flower from a smooth-bark tree. Fallen flowers lay around the tree like snowflakes.

"Ben, what aren't you telling me?"

My dad put the flower to his nose and smelled. "I'm just not sure. I don't know if we're right together."

"You've got to be kidding. He's wonderful."

"We're just different."

"Everyone is different. Don't tell me you want someone just like you. You'd drive yourself crazy. Differences make it interesting."

"But some differences are too much."

"Like?"

My dad sighed. "He's negative. He wanted to have sex without a condom."

"And?"

"What do you mean . . . AND?"

"So, did you talk about it? It doesn't have to be a deal-breaker. I can testify that safe sex is great sex."

My dad didn't answer.

Anthony continued, "So, did you talk about it?"

My dad remained quiet.

Anthony cocked his head. "Wait a minute, he doesn't know, does he? Ben? You haven't told him?"

My dad started walking again. "I haven't found the right time. We're always safe. And then after that weekend," my dad paused, "he assumes that

I'm negative. He probably doesn't want to be with someone who's positive." My dad turned toward Anthony. "He asked me if I was . . . clean. "

Anthony groaned. "Sorry."

My dad cut in. His words were sharp. "That's right, I'm dirty, and it's the kind of dirt you can never clean up."

"That is such a cruel word. But Ben, you haven't really given him a chance. Lots of negative guys are just clueless about what it's like to be positive. I've said lots of stupid stuff in my day, but thankfully I have friends who call me on it. You don't know if he has issues with being with someone who's positive. You haven't told him."

"And give him the chance to reject me? Why would I? I've done this disclosure thing. You haven't. Even the guys who don't outright run are changed by the conversation. You can feel the warmth and interest fade even as they maintain their calm good manners. I know people get rejected all the time for all kinds of reasons — too skinny, too fat, too hairy. But you can't catch fat or skinny or hairy. I think some guys secretly wish that Lyndon LaRouche had been successful in getting us all quarantined."

"I don't think Mike is like that. Isn't it worth taking a chance?"

"I have to bare my soul and tell someone I'm just getting to know about things that makes me feel totally exposed and vulnerable. It's not just that I'm positive. It's the whole story; how I got it, the secrets, the shame, the fear of getting sick, death. Why do I have to go there?"

"I know it's hard, but I think you're selling both yourself and him short. He seems like a really good guy. I bet he'd be OK."

"Let's talk about something else."

"Ben, don't do anything rash. Think about it. You've been so happy since he's been in the picture."

"Yeah, that was probably stupid of me."

We reached the park, and I ran ahead to say hello to all the dogs. As I made the rounds, I came upon a thick black-and-brown dog with a powerful head. I trotted over to say hello. The dog was on a tight leash, and a skinny human looked at me with big eyes and shook his head. I thought it a little strange, since dogs at this park don't wear leashes, but my tail overrode any hesitation. I was about to rub noses when something flashed in front of my face.

Something foul and bitter bubbled up from my stomach and stuck in my throat, and I realized the flash was snarling teeth. I tasted something metallic in my mouth, and red began to drip from my lip. I knew I wouldn't win this fight, but I also knew that I couldn't lose. From somewhere deep inside I found fight I never knew I had. I opened my mouth wide and clamped down on the dog's thick neck. He shook his powerful upper body and sent me tumbling on the grass. He leaped on top of me, hard sharp teeth flying at me from all directions. I squirmed under his heavy body and dodged as many of the attacks as I could. He was aiming for my throat.

"GET YOUR DOG." From the snarl of ugly dog voices I heard Anthony. "GET YOUR DAMN DOG!" Anthony was waving his big arms and shouting. Human hands and feet were grabbing and kicking. I saw Anthony's foot fly past my head and land on the other dog's stomach. There was a loud yelp. I broke free and ran. Out of the corner of my eye I saw my dad frozen, hands over his face. Anthony was kicking the other dog.

The skinny human was pulling hard on his dog's leash, trying to get him away from Anthony. "STOP. Leave my dog alone," the human yelled.

Anthony stopped and was breathing hard. "How dare you bring this . . . monster to a dog park?"

My dad looked like he was waking up and ran toward me. He dropped to his knees and wrapped his arms around me. I whimpered and nuzzled my nose into his face. I couldn't stop shaking.

"Sweetie, are you OK? You're safe now." Water dripped from my dad's eyes as his hand carefully slid over my body. Oh no, you're bleeding." His fingers moved slowly around my face. "Anthony, he's bleeding!"

"I'm calling the police." Anthony shook his fist at the human and dog. "That dog needs to be . . ."

The stocky dog was growling. His human held on to his collar. "He can't help it. He's a rescue. I just got him from the pound. Sorry."

"Is Beau OK?" Anthony yelled to my dad.

"I think so. I think it's just his lip."

The human and his dog started to walk away. Anthony shouted, "Stop, I want your name and phone number." The human started to run, pulling his dog with him. Anthony looked at my dad. "Should I chase them?"

My dad shook his head.

"You sure? I'd be happy to grab both of them by their necks." Anthony bent down and patted my head. "You were ferocious, little one. You showed that bully."

Sniffles were coming from my dad. "Let's just go home."

Anthony put his arm around my dad. "Sure, Ben, let's go."

Still shaking, I let my dad pick me up.

As we walked down the sidewalk my dad held me carefully. "I hope this doesn't change him."

Anthony reached over and patted my head. "No way. If any being knows who he is, Beau does!"

My dad continued, "I just don't want him to get mean . . . or scared."

Anthony shook his head. "Don't worry. He'll bounce back. No bully is going to take away this one's wiggle."

# Chapter 16

# Water-That-Never-Ends

I was sprawled out in a sunspot near my dad's feet. The talking-machine ring didn't even raise my head. The sun made me lazy but I couldn't sleep, because just as I started to bake in its heat, the spot would move and then, before long, I was outside of its sunny circle. I had been following these warm beds as they moved around the house all morning.

"Hello."

"Oh, hi, Mike."

"Yeah, it's a gorgeous day but I'm not feeling so great."

"It's probably nothing, just end-of-the-school-year exhaustion. I'm going to lay low today."

"Thanks, but I can't think of anything I need. I went to the store yesterday when I got home from work."

"That would be great. Beau would love an outing with Farrah. You know how he loves Fort

Funston, and it might actually be warm at the coast today."

"Yeah, I think he's mostly recovered from the attack. He might be a little more cautious, but that's probably a good thing."

I stretched from paw to paw so that I could touch as much of the sun as possible. The warmth started at the tips of each hair and worked its way down to untouched skin. I rolled over on my back and surrendered my pink belly. My eyelids drooped in that wonderful heavy place between sleep and awake.

"Noon would be great."

"Thanks."

"OK, see you soon."

I barely noticed the talking-machine click.

"Beau, wanna go to the beach with Farrah and Mike?"

I opened one eye.

"Wanna play BALL?"

My head shot up and I shook off the lazy sun. I ran to the drawer where my dad hid my ball and danced.

"I'll take that as a yes," my dad smiled.


"HAVE A GREAT time." My dad stood at the doorway as Mike led me and Farrah down the front steps.

The sun was everywhere. The sky was cloudless and blue. The sun slid off green leaves and bounced on the sidewalk.

"Wish you were coming with us." Mike looked at my dad as he walked backward down the steps."

"Another time." My dad crossed his arms. "Where'd you park?"

"Just around the corner on Scott Street."

"Bring back a story."

"Oh, with these two, you know there'll be a story," Mike chuckled.

We headed down the sidewalk and walked toward Mrs. Harris' house. I had not seen her in a very long time. During the cold and rain, she was never outside. But today she stood in front of her house, playing with her potted plants. As we got closer I saw that she was standing in the middle of a three-sided cage with wheels. Her shoulders were slumped.

"Hey, stop it, Beau," Mike said sharply. "Where do you think you're going?"

Mrs. Harris's head turned slowly toward us but seemed to get stuck midway. Her body stiffened. I barked.

"Good morning," she called out without looking at us.

Mike looked around and then saw Mrs. Harris. "Oh, good morning, ma'am, how are you today?'

"Moving slow but I'm blessed. How's my little friend?"

At the sound of Mrs. Harris's voice I made a quick dart and the leash fell from Mike's hand. I raced toward Mrs. Harris and ran around her rolling cage, jumping and dancing.

"Beau, no, OFF," Mike shouted as he rushed after me. "I'm sorry, ma'am. Beau, shame on you. Get over here."

I circled Mrs. Harris once more and then sat down by her feet to wait.

"It's OK, on a day like this I'd run and jump if I could. I just got out of the hospital, so it's nice to see so much energy. I haven't seen Beau for months."

Mrs. Harris slowly reached down and patted my head. Her other hand was stiff and shaking. "Look at you, all grown up."

She slowly reached into a pocket and then lowered her hand. Carefully, I licked the sweet crumbs in her palm.

"I've missed you, sweetheart," she said and then looked at Mike and Farrah.

Farrah was sitting next to Mike, shaking with excitement. She was better at waiting.

"So, Beau, who are your new friends?" Mrs. Harris asked.

"I'm Mike and this is Farrah," Mike answered.

"Nice to meet you. I'm Doris Harris." Mrs. Harris reached into her pocket. "Can she have a cookie?"

"Sure." Mike dropped Farrah's leash. "OK, Farrah, go ahead."

Farrah ran over and sat next to me. I moved closer to Mrs. Harris's feet.

"Sweetie, we've got to share with friends. Here you go." Mrs. Harris handed Farrah a treat. I nuzzled her pocket. "Oh, OK, you can have another one."

"Thanks," Mike said as he picked up our leashes. "That's enough, you two. We should get going."

Mrs. Harris looked down the street and asked, "Is Ben out of town?"

"No, he's feeling a little under the weather."

"Oh, I'm sorry. Tell him that he's in my prayers."

"I will. It was nice meeting you. Thanks again for the treats."

Mrs. Harris smiled. "Are you Ben's new friend?"

Mike shifted on his feet and turned slightly pink. "Uh, well, yeah."

"That's nice."

Mike was red and smiling. "You have a great day now."

"You too. Bye Beau, bye Farrah, hope to see you soon."

We followed Mike as he continued to walk down the sidewalk. I walked, looking backwards at Mrs. Harris. She was singing as she pushed her cage toward a pot of purple flowers.

"Come on, Beau, let's get to the beach." Mike gave my leash an easy tug.


I CAN ALWAYS sense it, long before we're there. There is something about that fishy, salty, bubbling, crashing, cold water that calls my name before we arrive. Farrah and I paced back and forth in the back of Mike's four-wheels, whining and staring out the window.

"Jeez, you two are both crazy. We're almost there." Mike called back at us.

The wheels slowed and then came to a stop. We both knew that the water was at the bottom of a long steep sandy path with stairs. Once out of four-wheels we leaned into our leashes, trying to hurry Mike.

I love everything wet. I love the rain, snow, puddles, my water bowl, and even baths. But there's something special about this water. It goes on for as far as I can see. I don't think it ever ends.

Farrah and I were pulling so hard that I almost missed the jingle of an approaching dog. Ever since that scary day in the park, I was a little more selective about whom I said hello to. The jingle got louder, and I saw a dark-red long-legged dog moving toward us. She had hair flowing from her legs and chest like me, but she was much taller. She wasn't connected to her leash and she didn't walk, she pranced. Farrah pulled toward Prancer. I sat and watched them sniff and then wag.

"Beau, she looks friendly." Mike looked at the woman with Prancer. "Hi, how's it going?" He pointed to me. "He's a little shy."

The woman had long legs and a curvy top. Her curly brown hair was pulled into a pile on top of her head. "Don't worry, Taffy's a love." She bent down and looked at me. She clapped her hands which made her fleshy top jiggle. "Come here, love, we just want to say hello." Her voice dipped and skipped.

I ran over to her outstretched hands.

"Oh, he's a doll. Come here, Taffy, say hello. What's his name?"

"Beau . . . and the other one's Farrah." Mike answered.

Taffy trotted over with Farrah. Taffy wagged while I carefully smelled her butt to see what she had for dinner last night. Then I smelled her mouth. She had a good breakfast.

The woman stood and winked at Mike. "See, we're all friends."

Mike suddenly found his pink color again. He laughed a strange laugh.

The woman smiled. "My name is Wendy."

Mike held out his hand. "Hi, I'm Mike."

I charged toward Taffy and shook my head to see if she wanted to chase me. Farrah barked.

"I think they want to play." The woman smiled bigger. "I don't think I've ever seen you here. I never forget a handsome face."

"I get here when I can. I live in the city."

"Well, you've got sweet dogs."

"Thanks. Farrah's mine. Beau is my, um, boyfriend's dog."

"Oh," the woman paused, "I see. Well, I should let you get down to the beach. It's great today. Enjoy. Come on, Taffy, let's go."

"Nice meeting you, Wendy, bye Taffy." Mike gave our leashes a tug. He quietly chuckled as we walked away.

Once at the stairway, he released our leashes and we tore off down the hill. At the bottom the water-that-never-ends was before us. There was white foam, greenish-blue water, and blue-black as it got deeper. Sand squeaked between my toes and my pads softened, surrounded by heat. As we got closer to the water the sand became firm and cool. We ran faster. Farrah got to the water first. Her long legs hopped over the first waves with a splash. I charged behind, quickly feeling the water rise to my belly. Soon my paws lifted and the water-that-never-ends held me in her arms. I held my head high as my legs ran without the thud of sand beneath my paws. A wave appeared from nowhere and tossed me toward the shore. When I got my feet underneath me, I ran back for more.

"SO HOW WAS IT?" my dad asked as we ran through the front door. "They aren't even wet? Where's all the sand?" My dad was wrapped in his long robe.

"I let the sun dry them and then they got brushed."

"Thanks."

My dad and Mike followed us to the eating-room. We ran to the water bowl. We took turns until it was all gone.

"They had a blast." Mike smiled. "They are both definitely water rats."

My dad smiled but looked sad.

Mike continued, "They swam like fish, chased each other, chased the ball, met some horses, and dug sandcastles. It doesn't get any better."

Farrah and I collapsed together on the rug.

My dad sat down at the table. "And you? Meet any interesting dog owners?"

"I didn't have time to look with these two." Mike grinned. "Are you trying to get rid of me? Why would I look when I can touch?" Mike wrapped his arms around my dad and then ran his hand through my dad's hair. "Oh, but I was hit on by someone with big boobs."

"The truth comes out. What was his name?"

"Wendy, if you must know." Mike chuckled.

"Hmmm," my dad replied.

"Oh, I also met your neighbor. Sweet lady. She told me to tell you that you're in her prayers."

"Prayers? Why?" my dad asked sharply.

I raised my head to see the change. Farrah snored softly.

Mike wrinkled his face. "I told her you weren't feeling well."

"Gee, thanks. I'm not sick."

"Sorry, I didn't know it was a secret."

"It's not, but I'm just not sick. I'm tired and exhausted."

"I didn't mean to hit a nerve. She just asked about you, and we were making small talk."

My dad sounded softer. "Sorry, I didn't mean to go off on you."

Mike continued, "Did you know that she just got out of the hospital?"

"I should call her. She had a stroke last month. She likes to get in my business but mostly in a good way. She's the good kind of Christian, the kind that doesn't preach. I should let her know that I'm fine or otherwise she will try to bring over one of her green bean and tater tot casseroles. They're delicious but I'm the one that should bring her something."

"Are you feeling worse?" Mike asked.

"Yeah, maybe a little."

"Do you need anything? I won't offer to cook anything because I want you to get well. But I'm really good at take-out. There's a hole in the wall Chinese restaurant in the Sunset that makes some really good Won Ton Soup."

"I've got some soup in the freezer."

"How about some fruit, tea, juice?"

"No, I'm good."

"Backrub?" Mike smiled. "Don't worry I can make it professional . . . well, maybe just a few extras."

My dad shook his head. "Really, I'm OK."

"Should I run out and get some movies? We could snuggle and watch some old ones."

"I prefer to be sick alone."

Mike was quiet. I watched him look hard at my dad. "You mean you want me to leave? I thought we'd hang out and I'd be your nurse."

"I'm not very good company right now."

"I wish you'd let me help. I want to take care of you. Ben, I really care about you." Mike's eyes started to get watery. "I think I am falling for you, Mr. Walker."

My dad sighed.

Mike quickly added, "You don't have to say anything back. I know you're not feeling well."

"Mike, I think I need some space. You're a great guy but I'm in a weird place."

"OK, OK, I hear you. I know everybody does sick differently."

"Actually, I might mean more than that. I'm feeling a little cornered. It's not you. It's me."

"Cornered?"

"I'm just . . . it doesn't feel like the right time."

"Don't shut me out. I get it that this isn't the time to talk about this. Let's talk when you feel better."

My dad sighed again. "Mike, I'm HIV positive."

Mike was silent.

My dad looked away. "We're just in different places."

"How come you didn't say something sooner? I thought you were negative."

"That's what I mean . . . we're in different places."

"I need to process this, but it doesn't mean that I'm going to dart out the back door."

"I think we just look at the future differently."

"Are you sick? I mean, do you have AIDS?"

"I've been kind of avoiding my doctor. My health has been good, but I quit the meds. I'm in some uncharted territory."

"Oh."

"I'm just not in the right place to think about a serious relationship."

"So, are you breaking up with me?"

My dad took a deep breath. "I don't know. I don't want to lose you, but I don't know how to do this. I just don't know how to navigate this myself, let alone with someone."

"I'm not sure what 'this' is, but let's talk about it when you're feeling better." Mike kissed the top of my dad's head. "I'll let you rest."

"Yeah, that's probably a good idea. Sorry for all of this."

"I'm not sure what you're sorry for, but I'm not going anywhere." Mike turned to leave. "Call me if you need something."

"Thanks."

Farrah got up and stretched. She put her nose in my face. I yawned and got up too. We followed Mike as he headed to the front door. My dad stayed in the eating-room.

Mike opened the front door. "Bye, Beau. We had lots of fun today." Mike's eyes were misty. He patted me on the head.

When the door closed, the house seemed very quiet. I heard my dad move to the sleeping-room. I got there in time to see him climb into his bed and pull the covers over his head. I didn't really want to go to bed. I didn't want Farrah to leave. I wasn't ready for the day to end. My pillow was lumpy and lonely. I tried to paw it, dig it like the sand at the beach. I dug faster and harder, trying to make my pillow right.

"HEY, Beau, stop it." My dad's voice was grumpy and hard.

I lay down with a big sigh, lumps and all.

# Chapter 17

## Wind

My dad sat and stared at the talking-machine. He wasn't talking. I watched and waited. Outside the wind howled, windows rattled, and scrawny branches scratched the house. Nothing happened. I whined. He still stared. I put my head in his lap and looked up. He didn't move but a drop of water tumbled off his chin and landed on his chest. Several other drops followed. I pushed my head deeper in his lap. Without looking, his hand found me and lay limp on my head. He took a shallow breath and finally looked down at me.

"Not good news, little one." His fingers began to make short trips along the crown of my head.

The rest of the morning took many wrong turns. He didn't rush out the door with his gone-till-supper-bag. He didn't move slow and easy, steaming cup in one hand, paper in the other, wearing his home-all-day fluffy robe. He moved like he was sleeping and couldn't wake up. When it was my time to pee and poop he just opened up the back door.

"Hurry up," he shouted as the wind grabbed his words and sent them flying.

I ran outside and darted around the backyard, chasing smells. Leaves swirled around like birds that had lost their way. The grey wind held water without making rain.

My dad yelled from the door, "HURRY UP, Beau."

I lifted my leg at the base of the tree and then ran over to the soft dirt and squatted.

MY DAD AND Anthony sat across from each other in the sitting-room.

"Sorry you made the trip over for nothing. I should've called and told you I was home sick." My dad was still in his sleeping clothes.

I sat by Anthony and leaned into his leg, "I would have still come over. I love my walks with the little buttercup." Anthony paused, "I thought there was an intruder when I heard you in the bedroom. It's always so quiet here when I get Beau." I leaned harder, hoping Anthony would get up and take me for our walk. He reached down and petted me. "You wouldn't know an intruder if you met one, would you? Everyone is just a potential ball thrower."

My ears perked up. No one made any move to look for a ball. I started to pace between Anthony and my dad. Outside the wind teased me with its bluster, sudden silence, and then whooshing whirl.

"The fog out there is thick and nasty today," Anthony announced and then looked sternly at my dad, "So why are you home? Why didn't you go to work?"

"I should've never signed up to teach summer school. What was I thinking? I was exhausted in May," my dad answered.

"You should've taken the summer off."

"I know. I thought I could just push through it."

"Is everything OK?" Anthony looked intensely at my dad.

My dad closed his eyes and sighed. "Promise me that you won't try and fix it."

"How could I ever promise that?" I plopped down by Anthony's feet and nudged him with my head. He started to rub my nose.

My dad looked at the floor. "Well, try. I'm looking for support not advice."

"Come on, Ben, stop talking around whatever it is. Just tell me."

"OK, but hear me out."

"OUT WITH IT."

"I got a call from my doctor this morning."

"Shit."

"My labs aren't good."

"How bad?"

"Twelve . . . T cells," my dad said slowly.

Anthony stopped rubbing me and stared at my dad.

My dad's voice was soft. "My viral load is off the charts."

Anthony moaned. "Shit. This didn't have to . . . if you hadn't stopped taking your meds."

My dad watched Anthony and then said softly, "Maybe, but if I had to do it over again, I'm not sure I'd do anything different."

"So are you back on meds?"

My dad looked out the window. "No."

"WHAT?" Anthony shouted as he leaned forward.

I started to run around the room. Anthony's rising voice matched a swell in the rustling leaves on the other side of the wall.

Anthony stood up. "Are you insane? Or is it that you just have a death wish?"

My dad got up and started to walk out of the room. "I'm not having this conversation."

I ran after my dad.

Anthony followed. "Too bad, it's a conversation you need to have. Ben, the meds could bring your numbers back up."

My dad stopped and faced Anthony. "But at what cost?"

I ran back to Anthony. "Are you kidding? The protease inhibitors are saving lives. Do you know how many obituaries there were in the *Bay Area Reporter* last week? Eight! They used to fill up two entire pages."

"I don't want to live life in a bathroom."

"But you don't know when they'll find better meds. Look how far they've come."

My dad shook his head. "All you can think about is living, as if life only requires the will to live. No matter how much we choose life, all roads eventually lead us to the same place."

"But not before we're supposed to."

"Oh, and I guess you know when we're supposed to."

Anthony held up his hands. "Ben, stop it."

"I'm thirty-five years old, I'm not supposed to live life in diapers. You think it's suicidal. I think it's making a choice. I'm not choosing to die. I'm choosing to live . . . on my terms." My dad was breathing hard.

I ran over to my dad and jumped up on his leg, but his eyes didn't move away from Anthony. Anthony looked back and then away.

"I don't want to lose you." Anthony's big shoulders started to make tiny shakes.

My dad sighed. "Come here." He held his arms open.

Anthony fell into my dad's arms and whimpered.

My dad stroked his hair. "It's going to be alright. You aren't going to lose me."

I ran around them, barking, and then ran to the front door and back. Anthony sniffled into my dad's neck.

"Beau needs to go out," my dad said. "Let's go for a walk. Judy's coming over later, could you stay? I can't face her alone."

"OK," Anthony said quietly.


THE DOORBELL rang. I was in the middle of my after-walk nap. Anthony and my dad were napping too, snuggled together in the sitting-room. I jumped up and started to bark. The doorbell rang again. My dad got up and moved slowly toward the door. The bell rang again. He put his eye up against the door and sighed.

When he opened the door I raced out. "Hi Judy," my dad said.

With one hand Judy held onto a scarf wrapped around her head. She waved the other hand high. Her fingernails were bright red. The long ends of the scarf flapped around her like wings. I barked and danced at Judy's feet.

"It's freezing out here. What took you so long?"

"I had to make sure you weren't the Jehovah's Witness," my dad smiled.

"Are you kidding, you've got a rainbow flag. You can't be saved."

"You'd be surprised how often they try."

Judy bent down. "Hello, precious, no, I haven't forgotten you." She rubbed my wiggling butt. She looked up at my dad. "How was work today?"

"I stayed home and hung out with Anthony."

Judy stood up and cocked her head. "Must be nice. Some of us have to work."

"I just needed a mental health day. Come on in."

Anthony's voice rang out from deep inside the house, "Is it her? Give me a minute to hide the toys. You know how she is!"

Judy looked at my dad and rolled her eyes. She shouted down the hallway, "Yes, dear, it's me. And don't you worry, I have no interest in any of your toys."

My dad kissed Judy's cheek. "Thanks for coming over."

"You should have warned me that HE would be here, I would have told the salon to sharpen my nails."

"Come on. I'll make some coffee."

"I'd love something stronger than coffee."

My dad smiled. "I'm guessing Anthony is already in the kitchen with an opened bottle of wine and is drinking from the bottle as we speak."

"Well, on that ONE point Anthony and I agree," Judy said as they both walked back to the eating-room.

Anthony was sitting on the counter with his legs pulled up to his chest. He had a glass in one hand and a bottle in the other. "Hi, dear, I hope you don't mind if I stay up here. I'm afraid of snakes."

Judy showed her teeth and hissed at Anthony.

"Come on you two, kiss, kiss," my dad scolded.

Judy moved toward Anthony as their heads tilted in opposite directions. "Muah," they both said. Then they tilted their heads the other way. "Muah," they said again.

"How are you, Nurse Ratchet?" Judy asked. "I can see they haven't locked you up with the patients yet."

Anthony smiled, "Nope, another day of freedom." He handed her a glass filled with red.

"Cheers," they said as their glasses clinked.

"So what's up, Ben?" Judy nodded at Anthony. "Anytime you want to talk to both of us, there is some . . ." Judy paused, "unveiling."

My dad moved over to the table and sat down.

"I hate sit-down conversations." Judy held out her hand to Anthony. "Come on, twinkle toes. Let's get this over."

I trotted with them to the table. When they sat down, they forgot about me. I ran from chair to chair. Judy looked at my dad. My dad looked at Anthony. Anthony looked at his glass.

My dad cleared his throat. "In the interest of not keeping secrets, I have something to tell you."

"I don't like the sound of this." Judy's tone changed.

Anthony remained silent.

"I told Anthony earlier today." My dad bit his lower lip. "I got some bad news from my doctor." He paused. "My labs have taken a downturn. I hoped it was a lab error, but they repeated the tests and things aren't good."

Judy looked at my dad and then Anthony. "But there are new meds, right. I've been reading about them in the *Chronicle*."

My dad continued. "I was on them, but I stopped several months ago because they made me sick."

"Well, can't you go back on them?"

Anthony looked up from his glass and into my dad's face.

My dad looked away. "I don't want to."

Judy cocked her head toward Anthony. "What does that mean?"

The wind howled but no one spoke. I started to bark.

"Beau, STOP IT." My dad shouted. He got up and got me a bone.

I took the bone to my pillow. I held my bone between my front paws. My teeth slid across the smooth hard surface that murmured encouragement with each scrape.

Anthony looked at Judy. "A high viral load means that the virus is replicating, and his low T cells mean he doesn't have much of an immune system. He's at serious risk for opportunistic infections — serious ones like KS and pneumocystis, the ones that took so many people in the '80s. For the record, I told him he was crazy to stop taking the meds. And I don't understand why he doesn't restart them now."

Judy shook her head. "No, no, no, you can't do this, Ben." Her eyes filled with water.

"I'm taking supplements and working with a nutritionist. Not everyone believes in the medications. There are lots of success stories with natural remedies. It makes more sense to me. The meds feel like poison. You don't have any idea how bad they made me feel—tired all the time, constantly going to the bathroom, messed-up sleep, depressed, my head felt like it was in a fog."

"Who says the meds caused all that?" Anthony asked.

"Well, I only know that I felt better when I stopped."

Judy wiped the corner of her eyes. "But it could be your life we're talking about?"

"That's the privilege of the healthy, you think that if you get sick you can always do something to make you well. When I was on meds, it didn't feel like a life."

"This feels like quitting." Judy looked at my dad and then Anthony.

"I know you want me to be a fighter. You'd like me to be one of those HIV poster boys on bus stops but they aren't real. Those poster models aren't sick. They don't have AIDS wasting in their faces or buffalo humps on their backs. Hope is sexy. AIDS is not."

Back and forth my dad, Judy, and Anthony argued. Against the grinding of my bone and the whoos and shhhh of the wind, the human voices became a dull hum.


CHAIRS WERE sliding across the floor. I looked up from my bone.

"I don't get it. It makes no sense. It makes me mad and it scares me. But whatever your decision,

Ben, don't cut me out. I want to be here even if I disagree." Anthony sounded very tired.

My jaw was aching and my mouth was dry.

Judy's face was puffy and her eyes were red. "You know I love you, for better or worse. I usually want to wring your neck but it's because I love you." Judy wrapped her arm around my dad's arm. "Please think about this."

The wind had stopped blowing. My bone showed no signs of my hard work. There wasn't even a dent.

# Chapter 18

# Morning that Wasn't

I know things change. Usually, I love the adventure. But when I get used to something, when something good happens day after day, I can't help it — I start to count on it.

I yawned, stretched, and walked around my dad's bed, sat and waited. After many gray mornings, this one looked like it could be brighter. The sun peeked behind the heavy sun-stealer that hung over the window. Slivers of white snuck out the sides of the heavy cloth. My dad had tossed and turned all night, throwing off the blankets and then wrapping up in them. I got up. My nails clicked loudly on the hard floor as I walked around to the other side. My dad's head didn't pop out of the mound of blankets. I sighed and sat down. No hand slid out of the heap to pat my head. I whined.

"Shit," my dad moaned.

He curled into a ball and pulled the blankets tighter. I made a cry that ended with a bark. The blankets rustled and my dad's feet dropped to the floor as he sat up. He pulled one of the blankets around him. His body shook and his hair was wet and wild. There were no friendly words. He slowly stood up and shuffled out of the sleeping-room with his blanket dragging behind him. I followed. I was confused but happy that the day was going to get started. He walked down the hallway and through the eating-room. He opened the back door and just stood there with the door wide open.

"Out, go outside," my dad nodded to the outside. "Go," he said more sharply. He pointed outside. "GO."

I ran outside and heard the door slam behind me. I quickly peed and pooped. There were no happy words of encouragement. I ran back to the door and barked. The door opened but instead of morning sounds, my dad just walked away. A familiar smell wafted across the room.

My food bowl had somehow filled. My dad always announced it was eating time with the rattle and ping-pong of kibble falling into my bowl. I darted over and gobbled up every nugget. Once the crunching stopped, it was very quiet. My dad wasn't sitting at the table with his cup, papers, and music. I was alone. I ran to each room and found him in the sleeping-room. He was back in his bed.

Wasn't this morning? I stood and watched him. He groaned but then grew quiet. My full belly made my eyes heavy, so I plopped down on my pillow too. Morning could come later. Just as I was beginning to close my eyes, the talking-machine rang out. My dad's hand appeared from under the pile and reached for the machine.

"Hello," he said hoarsely. "Hey, Judy."

"Summer school is over."

"I don't feel so good. I think it's the flu."

My dad groaned.

"I get these cramps and I must have a fever. I was hot and cold all night."

"No, Mike's not here. We're still kind of taking a break."

"I know you like him."

"You don't have to come over."

"OK, sure, if it's not a hassle. I don't have an appetite but maybe later. And Beau could use a walk."

"Thanks. Just let yourself in."

My dad put down the machine and crawled back under the blankets. Before either of us got settled the machine rang again.

"What, Judy?"

"Sorry, Anthony, I was just talking to Judy."

My dad started shaking.

"It's the flu."

"No, I haven't called my doctor."

"I should've guessed Judy would call you."

"I'm not in denial." My dad held his tummy and groaned. "Just a minute."

"Yes I'm still here. I get these cramps."

"The usual flu symptoms—fever, aches and pains, stomach crap, and I'm so tired."

"Of course I'm worried, but what good does that do? It doesn't make me feel better."

"Anthony, I'm not in the mood to talk about this. I just need to sleep."

"Fine, come over. You know Judy's coming too."

"OK, me too. Bye."

My dad pulled the blankets back over his head.

I WOKE WITH a jerk to the sound of clinking metal at the front door. I was confused. I had lost track of the day.

My dad didn't move. I jumped up, barking, and ran to the door. The door slowly opened. Judy and Anthony were standing in sunshine. I jumped up and down.

"We're here," Anthony called out. "We'd be here sooner if someone didn't drive like she was a blue-haired old lady."

Judy bent low to rub me. "You know what, sweet pea, I think your big friend here is walking home." I inhaled Judy's sweet flower smell. "So are you taking good care of the patient?" My nose moved to the bags. "Hey, stay out of there. That's for your dad."

I ran down the hallway and back again.

"Get over here, crazy child. I've got something for you." Anthony reached into his pocket and pulled out a chew. I sat by his feet and smacked my lips. "Here you go, chew your little heart out."

"Ben, where are you?" Judy started down the hallway.

"In bed," my dad called from the sleeping-room.

I ran ahead. Judy and Anthony followed. My dad was sitting up.

"Hey," my dad ran his hand over his hair. "Don't look, I'm a mess."

Judy and Anthony sat down on the bed and silently watched my dad. I took a running jump and landed in the middle of them all.

"Have you lost your mind? Beau, get off the bed." My dad pushed me off, and I landed with a thud, my chew still in my mouth.

Anthony smiled, "I can see your attendant is taking good care of you." He reached down and rubbed my ears. "It's OK, sweetheart, he's not very good at letting anyone help."

"I brought you some Matzo ball soup from that deli on Polk Street," Judy announced.

"Thanks, maybe later."

"You can try some broth."

"I don't have much of an appetite right now."

"You can try."

My dad looked at Judy and sighed. "OK."

"This place is a mess." Judy started to pick up clothes on the floor.

"Judy, you don't need to . . ."

"Stop." Judy held up her hand. "You need to let us help."

She moved quickly around the room, putting clothes in a basket and collecting glasses and dishes. She walked out of the sleeping-room with the bags and a stack of dishes. My dad lay back down.

"She's a good egg." Anthony continued to sit on the bed. "She's a bit cracked but her heart's in the right place. Lord knows, she and I have had our ups and downs, but things are better. I'm not sure why but it's easier."

My dad closed his eyes and made a little smile. "I've noticed. I'm glad."

Judy's voice yelled from the eating-room. "Hey, only one of you is sick, so the other one better get in here and help."

"I didn't say that SHE was easy," Anthony chuckled and then yelled back, "Coming, sweetheart."

I trotted after Anthony into the eating-room. Judy was opening and closing cabinet doors, banging pots, and clanging dishes. When we came into the room, she stopped and looked at Anthony. Her eyes were big and shiny.

"Should I be worried?" Judy whispered.

"I'm not sure. I think we need to talk him into going to the ER. I hope it's not anything serious. I pray that it's not something like MAC."

"What's that?"

"Mycobacterium avium complex. It's a bacterial infection. People with AIDS and low T cells are susceptible. It's ugly, but it's more treatable than it used to be."

Judy shook her head. "How do you do it? You've seen so many with this awful disease. How do you keep going? How do you even get up in the morning with everything you've seen?"

"It's the reason I DO get up. It's for them. They've taught me most of my important life lessons. I have to get up. Someone has to bear witness, someone has to know their stories." Anthony's eyes started to glisten.

"You've seen so many die."

Anthony nodded his head. "Yeah, too many."

A tear rolled down Judy's cheek. "He's not going to . . ."

Anthony put his arms around Judy. "Don't go there. We just need to get him to see a doctor."

Judy rubbed the back of her hand over her eyes. "OK, then, let's give him some soup and some tough love."

They filled a tray with steaming wonderful smells. "Here comes medicine only a Jewish mother could make," Judy shouted.

"Or a really good deli," Anthony added.

My dad was sitting up again when we walked back into the sleeping-room. "You didn't need to."

Judy raised her hand.

"But I'm glad you did," my dad quickly added. "It smells great."

I ran from one side of the bed to the other, trying to get a better look and smell.

My dad had a few spoonfuls. "It's delicious but that's all I can eat."

Judy and Anthony looked at each other. Anthony spoke first. "Ben, we're taking you to the emergency room this afternoon."

"I'll be fine. I just need to rest."

"It's not a question," Judy said firmly. "We're taking you to get this checked out. Anthony is going to call ahead to Davies Medical Center. He knows the doctor who's on duty today."

My dad looked at Judy and then Anthony. "So this is what it feels like when you two are pushing in the same direction. I think I was safer when you were fighting."

"We're serious, Ben," Anthony said without a smile.

"Fine. You win," my dad sighed.


IT WAS STARTING to get dark when they came home. I was starving and had to pee.

"Hey, Beau," they all said together. Anthony and Judy stopped and gave me a good rub, but my dad walked on by.

"I'm going back to bed. I'm worn out." He turned back toward us. "I told you it wasn't anything."

"It *is* something. You heard the doctor, this flu is no joke." Anthony scolded.

"Yeah, I know." My dad paused. "Thanks. You know I appreciate both of your mothering — well, most of the time."

Judy waved her hand. "Go to bed. We'll take care of Beau and get you something to eat."

"Nothing for me, but go ahead and have some of the soup yourselves."

"OK, but I'll bring you some 7-Up," Judy replied.

Anthony clapped his hands toward me and headed toward the back door. "Come on, pipsqueak, let's go outside."

The day ended as strangely as it began. After Judy and Anthony ate and took care of me, they tiptoed out of the house and quietly closed the door. The house was dark. My dad snored softly. He never said goodnight.

# Chapter 19

# Warm Nights

All the windows of the house were open. A wind machine sat on the floor next to my bed. The whirling hum blew warm air across my face.

"Hey, Mike," my dad said into the talking-machine.

"I know. It's great to have some real summer even though we had to wait for September to get it. And with my leave from work, I actually get to enjoy it."

"Beau is camped out in front of the fan like an old man. I bet Farrah is hot, with all that hair."

"Lucky girl. What a great day go to Crissy Field. I bet she swam her little heart out. Was it warm enough for people to swim?"

"By the way, thanks for that talk the other day. I don't know how many friends would be willing to have that talk. Most people prefer denial."

"Don't worry, it's an academic interest. I'm not there, not even close. It's just good to talk about options, especially since they are taboo."

"Well, I'm grateful. Thank you."

"Are you going out tonight? I'm sure the Castro will be hopping with this weather. You know, boys and sultry nights."

"I can't. I'm getting together with Anthony and Judy."

"They're coming over for dinner."

There was a long silence. I opened my droopy eyes. My dad still held the talking-machine in his hands.

"Maybe we can get together later in the week. I really need to talk to them, and I think it's best if I do it alone."

"Have some fun tonight, Mike. You deserve it."

"OK. Talk to you soon."

"Bye."


I LOVE IT WHEN humans eat outside. There's nothing like fresh air and the hunt for food. My nose works better outside.

"Don't you just love our Indian summers. Almost makes up for all the fog." Anthony stretched in the warm night air.

Anthony, Judy, and my dad were sitting around the table on the deck with bare legs and naked feet. The air was not moving. The heat from the day surrounded us even though the sun had begun to disappear, leaving a pink sky. I searched the floor beneath the table, looking for fallen treats.

"That fish was amazing." Judy lifted her glass and drank.

The smoky smells had been promising something special all night.

"It was too warm to cook inside," my dad replied. "How often does that happen in San Francisco? Good night to BBQ. I got the fish at that seafood truck at the Civic Center farmer's market. I love their stuff and they've got great prices."

"How'd you think to wrap it in lettuce leaves?" Judy raised her fork to her mouth.

I waited for something to slip off and fall to the floor.

"I didn't know where to find fig leaves so I thought romaine might work." My dad chewed.

"Well, here's to another delicious meal." Anthony picked up his glass, and they all clinked their glasses together.

"And here's to your health." Judy added.

"Hear, hear," my dad said as he took a drink. "I'm finally feeling close to my old self. Well, almost; maybe I can now pursue that career as a runway model. I haven't weighed this much since I was in high school."

"More meals like this one, and you'll be back to your bear weight in no time." Anthony put more food on his plate.

"What a perfect night." Judy said. "Even that one," she pointed at Anthony, "is on good behavior."

"The heat makes me mellow, sweetie. It seems to have slowed your tongue, too." Anthony blew Judy a kiss.

My dad shook his head. "You two really should just get married."

"What? And destroy a perfectly good relationship?" Judy took another drink.

"Speaking of which, can you believe Clinton confessed? Do you think he could be impeached for a blow job?" Anthony asked wide-eyed.

"It's not the sex, it's that he lied." Judy shook her head. "I feel so bad for Hillary . . . and Monica too. Sadly, it seems so ordinary and predictable."

The eating noises started to slow, which is never a good sign. Treats don't fall if humans don't eat. They all looked up at the sky and breathed deeply and sat in silence.

My dad shifted in his chair. "You know, I've been thinking about something."

"Blow jobs?" Anthony smiled.

"Shut up. It's kinda serious." My dad sat up straighter.

"Please no more sex or politics," Judy whined.

My dad looked away.

Judy added, "You know I'm kidding. What's on your mind?"

"Well, that last bout with the flu kind of shook me up. I haven't been that sick in a long time."

Anthony looked at Judy and then my dad. "It scared us too."

My dad continued, "Well, it got me thinking about something. Remember all the paperwork the nurse gave me at the ER? One of the forms was a health directive."

I roamed from chair to chair, checking to see if I had missed any crumbs.

"My mom had one." Judy reached down and petted my head. "And she made sure I knew about it. As it turned out, I didn't have to make any decisions. After that last round of chemo, she went fast."

"I remember." My dad sounded sad. "That was so hard at the time, but now it seems like a blessing."

I walked over to Anthony and he picked me up and held me in his lap. "Health directives are a good idea. At Shanti I've seen what can happen when they aren't set up. Doctors and families end up making all kinds of decisions that aren't what the patient wanted."

My dad took a sip from his glass. "I think I want something more than a health directive. I want to make my own decision."

Anthony lifted my ears and let air move through the sweaty insides. "That's the whole point. You can state what kind of medical assistance you want, if you don't want to be resuscitated, if you don't want life support, if you . . ."

My dad interrupted. "I want to be able to choose the time."

"Time?" Anthony scrunched his face. "What are you talking about?"

It got quiet. The hum of wheels on nearby streets was barely noticeable. There was faint laughter from an open window somewhere in the neighborhood.

My dad folded his hands. "I want to ask you guys something, but I want you to think about it before you give me an answer. It's a big request."

Anthony and Judy stared at my dad.

"Would you help me? Would you help me if it gets to that point? Would you help me end it?"

Anthony and Judy looked away from my dad into the night sky.

"I'm feeling great, so I'm not talking about anything immediate. It's a theoretical question."

Judy frowned. "For the record, I don't like the question."

"Me neither," Anthony agreed. "But Ben, that's the purpose of palliative care. That's what hospice is all about. All of my clients at Shanti at some point make a decision to stop treatment and only take medicine that makes them comfortable. It's all about helping them make a good transition."

My dad crossed his arms and spoke more softly. "I don't mean something that the doctors can do. It would be something that only you could do."

Judy shook her head. "NO, absolutely not. I don't even want to hear you talking like this. I can't believe you're asking us to help you commit suicide. Suicide is a sin and assisted suicide is against the law!"

"It's not suicide. I'm just asking you to help speed up the process if I'm ever at a point where the end is inevitable and I can't end it myself. I'd do all the research ahead of time. Wouldn't you want help if you were ever in that place? Think about it—you're not going to get better, you're in pain, no quality of life, a burden on others, and you can't even end it! Wouldn't you want help?"

Judy looked hard at my dad. "No. It's the easy way out."

My dad stared back. "What's wrong with easy? I've had lots of hard. I'm not asking you to do this if I'm well. I'm talking about the potential of a long and painful death. It's not like I'd be cheating. It would just make it sooner rather than later."

Judy cocked her head. "Isn't that what your mom did?"

My dad tightened his lips and shook his head. "I can't believe you're going there. That not fair. It's not the same. She wasn't dying and she committed suicide."

"But she was suffering," Judy replied. "And I bet she thought it would never end."

"I'm not talking about ending my life because I'm unhappy. My mom could have gotten help. She should have seen a therapist. She could have gotten into recovery. She didn't even try."

Anthony's eyes glistened. "Well, I feel the same way about your refusal to take HIV meds."

"Forget it. I shouldn't have asked you." My dad got up and started stacking dishes. "You obviously don't understand."

Anthony moved to the edge of his chair. "Then help me understand. What's the difference between your mom refusing treatment and you refusing meds?"

"We've had this conversation. I'm telling you, HIV meds aren't a cure. And I've tried them. They don't make me feel better. If all they do is make me sick, then what's the point of prolonging life? The only ones who win in that scenario are the drug companies. I'm disappointed in you, Anthony. Given your work with hospice, I thought you'd understand."

Anthony picked up his glass and took a deep drink. "I think there are two issues here and they're getting mixed up. Ben, I might disagree with your decisions but I do support *you* making decisions about your health, life, and death. But that's very different from asking *me* to do it."

My dad picked up the stack of dishes and started walking toward the house. "Just think about it."

Warm nights never last very long. A breeze that started soft and warm was starting to bring coolness. It blew in from some mysterious place.

# Chapter 20

# Clouds Mean Rain

The rain was back. It was a cold and wet morning. The sun seemed to have lost its way. But as we started out on our walk, the water drops had a faint sparkle. Was it a hint of change?

It started with a cough. My dad smelled like rust and was moving slower.

"Hello, Mrs. Harris," my dad said as we walked past Mrs. Harris's house.

I pulled to get closer to Mrs. Harris. My dad had recently gotten a new leash, one that could grow or shrink. Sometimes I had lots of room to roam, and other times I got to the end after only a short wander.

"Good morning, Ben." Mrs. Harris bent down and gave me a rub. "Good morning, Beau. Are you going to the park to enjoy some sun?" She slowly stood up. "Looks like we might have a break in the weather."

"Yeah, I hope so. Although Beau doesn't care whether it's rain, sun, or fog."

"He must see possibility in all of them."

"You're right about that. I wish I had a dose of whatever he takes every morning." My dad smiled but then held his hand to his mouth as puffs of air escaped through his fingers.

"Dear, are you coming down with something?" Mrs. Harris asked.

"I think it's a cold," my dad replied. "Seems like everyone I know has one."

"Well, you be careful. I know schools are terrible for bugs. We don't want you getting sick."

"I'm actually on a leave of absence from my job." My dad put his hand to his mouth and coughed again. "I've been so exhausted lately. I decided to take a break."

"Good for you."

"I feel like I could sleep for a year."

"Maybe you should. Teaching was simpler in my day. I can only imagine the stress today."

My dad muffled another cough. "Enough about me, how have you been feeling? You look like you're getting around better."

"I am. I've graduated from the walker to a cane, and soon I think I'll be able to walk without the cane, so that's real progress. God is good," Mrs. Harris paused, "all the time."

"I'm glad. But I suspect that your doctor and all your hard work at physical therapy had something to do with it, too. Let's not give God all the credit."

"But I do." Mrs. Harris smiled.

"You have a wonderful attitude, Mrs. Harris."

"Oh, it's not me, Ben. I struggle like everyone. Believe me, I can be cranky and negative with the best of them. It's only because of God's grace. It's bigger than me. It says that everything will be OK even when it doesn't feel like it. Grace says I'm OK just as I am. You know that there is nothing that can separate us from God's grace. It's always sufficient and always right on time."

My dad was quiet.

"Oh, listen to me, you didn't stop to hear me preach."

My dad sighed. "It's OK. I admire your faith. I'm not used to people talking about God without talking about judgment."

"They're the things I wish I had told my son." Mrs. Harris looked far away. "The anniversary of his death is tomorrow." She leaned heavily on her cane. "I didn't understand my son, still don't, so I judged him. Parents do the best they can but it's usually not enough. I hope he had a sense of God's grace."

"I'm sure he knew that you loved him."

"I hope so, but the last time we talked he was high. I wasn't a very good example of grace."

"Addicts sometimes need love that is tough. You can't change an addict, they have to do that."

"With God's help." Mrs. Harris' smile returned. "It sure is good to see you, Ben."

"And I'm glad you're doing so much better." My dad gave my leash a tug. "We should get going before the rain comes back. Come on, Beau. Have a good day, Mrs. Harris."

"You feel better. Let me know if you need anything. You know you're always in my prayers."

"Thanks. Say good-bye, Beau."

We started off toward the park. The clouds were moving, making room for more sun. The air was fresh and washed but as we moved down the sidewalk, a funky smell began to call out my name.

A human carrying a black case, dressed in shiny shoes and a long black coat, was walking toward us. "Hey, how's it going?"

"Hey," my dad nodded as we met shiny-shoes.

"You might want to cross over to the other side." Shiny-shoes wrinkled his face. "There's a bum up ahead that stinks to high heaven. He's babbling on about something. This city's got to do something about the homeless."

"Uhh, thanks," my dad mumbled. Shiny-shoes walked past us shaking his head.

I quickened my pace and was happy with my new leash's extra freedom. I'm sure my dad didn't smell it coming. I don't think his nose ever worked. Gradually a human came into view. He was sitting on the sidewalk, bundled up in clothes and frantically rocking back and forth. I darted over to him before my dad could say no.

"It's gonna get you. It's gonna get you." He rocked over and over. He smelled like dirty wet clothes that never quite dry. The flesh that peeked out from his bulky layers was puffy and pink. I pushed my nose in his hairy face. He smelled more animal than human.

My dad pulled on my leash. "No, Beau. Sorry! BEAU, NO," he said louder.

The man looked at me with surprised eyes that quickly became soft as he slowed his rock to a gentle back and forth. "Hello, puppy," he said with a toothless smile. The smells that came out of his mouth were sour and rotten. "I used to have a puppy."

My dad relaxed the leash.

David A. Fredrickson	216

The man slowly looked up at the sky and his smile disappeared. "It's never enough. It'll get you when you sleep, when you're not looking. Alpha, Charlie, Tango, take cover. Protect yourself or you'll end up in the pit. They're coming. Hide." He pulled his hood over his head and buried his face into the bundle of rocking clothes.

My dad started to cough. He pulled my leash and started to walk away. "Come on, Beau, let's go."

There is no such thing as good smells or bad smells. They all are just smells. They're always interesting and sometimes they're important.

The sky was rearranging the clouds again. It began to push aside the sunlight, threatening rain. "We've got to hurry. Let's go, Beau." My dad started to walk quickly but then slowed, breathing heavy breaths between coughs. He stopped and looked backward. "Maybe we should go home." He looked forward. "Well, I guess we're almost there." We continued down the sidewalk toward the park.

The park was busy and the ground was wet. As my dad unclicked my leash, I tore off to explore. I looked back over my shoulder to make sure my dad was following. Instead, he sat down on a bench. I ran back to the bench and waited for him to get up. He was breathing hard.

"Not today, Beau, I feel like crap." My dad waved his hand. "Go play."

With hints of change, I sat down by his feet and waited. All my friends ran around the park like it was any other day. They couldn't smell it.

# Chapter 21

## Change

Over the next few days my dad's cough started to sound like crackling leaves, and he moved like he was pulling rocks. Our walks got shorter and shorter, and then they stopped. He started to do the back-door walks where the open door meant I would be going alone. And then sometimes he didn't even get around to opening the door. I had left a couple puddles in the house, and I don't think he even noticed. Daytime and nighttime became bedtime. Everything was a sleepy blur.

Finally, one chilly morning I heard the jingle of keys. I raced to the opening front door.

"BEN?" Anthony's voice boomed through the door. He saw me dancing at his feet. "Hey little buddy, what's up with your dad? He isn't answering the phone." He walked past me down the hallway without an ear rub. "Jeez, this place looks like a bomb went off. Ben, where are you?" Anthony stopped at the sleeping-room. "Ben?"

My dad didn't sit up. He coughed and then breathlessly said, "Might . . . need to see the doctor."

Anthony stepped over clothes lying on the floor and moved closer to my dad.

"Don't get too close."

"Are you kidding? I'm a nurse." Anthony put his hand on my dad's forehead. "Are you coughing up phlegm?"

"No . . . nothing comes up."

"Fever?"

"Yeah . . . probably."

"Night sweats?"

"Yeah."

"Why didn't you call? Why didn't you answer the phone?"

"I thought," my dad breathed hard, "I would get better."

Anthony shook his head. "I'm taking you to the hospital. We should pack a bag. I have a feeling they're going to admit you."

My dad answered with a long string of coughs.

MY DAD WAS gone for days. Anthony and Judy took turns staying with me. They didn't do anything right. They didn't know that I always do a sit-stay before I eat, they didn't know how to hide the ball under my bed and pretend like it's in another room, they didn't know that the screaming kettle on the stove scares me.

Then finally my dad came home. I couldn't wait for everything to get back to normal. I dropped my favorite ball by his bed. I shook my tug rope and growled. I ran up and down the hallway. But everything was different. He hardly even noticed my tricks. Days were filled with new people and the body smells humans usually try to keep private.

"How much can Hospice provide?" Anthony asked.

Judy, Anthony, and Mike sat at the eating-room table with a human dressed in loose green pants and white shoes. Around her neck she wore a Y-shaped rope with a shiny round on the end. My dad's chair was empty. I could hear the wheeze of the machine in the sleeping-room breathe in and out.

"Our primary goal is to make Ben comfortable. I should warn you, pneumocystis can be rough, but we'll do everything we can to make Ben comfortable. And we are here to support all of you in this process." White-shoes had soft eyes and a gentle voice.

All the wonderful smells of the eating-room had grown stale. The chopping, sizzling, steaming sounds of food were gone. Any treats I found on the floor were dropped from bags and cartons that made their way into our house without the usual building of food sounds and smells. They all were missing my dad's touch.

Anthony held a pad of paper. "How often can you come? We need to make a schedule so someone is always here."

"I'll be here every other day for a couple hours to check vitals, meds, or anything else the doctor might order. I'll also be on-call if anything unexpected comes up. A nursing aide will be here for general care. I can have him come on the days

I'm not here. We also have a social worker on staff. But it's all flexible as Ben's needs change."

Mike and Judy had tissues wadded in their hands, damp from tears. Anthony did all the talking. "What do we need to do?"

White-shoes looked at Anthony. "Since you're a nurse, I know you know this stuff." She looked at Judy and Mike. "It's pretty straightforward. He needs to be moved every couple of hours so he doesn't get bedsores. I'll show you an easy way to do that. Here's a med log to keep track of his meds. If he eats or drinks anything it should be logged. We're keeping track of input and output so you should write down the amount of urine in the bag if you empty it. And I'll show you how to replace the fluids in his IV. I'm always available by phone if you have any questions."

"Thank you," Anthony said.

White-shoes got up. "I'm going to check on Ben. I'll be here for another hour or so if you think of anything else." She walked out of the room.

Anthony looked at his paper. "There's a lot of time to cover. I'd suggest we do this week by week. Things might . . ." he paused, "change."

"I'm taking a family medical leave from work so you can schedule me as much as you need," Judy said quietly.

"I'm available on the weekends and evenings," Mike added.

Rain was splattering outside. It was an easy rain that could last a long time.

"It's really sweet of you to help," Judy said to Mike. "I know things with you and Ben never had the chance to . . . I know what it feels like when Ben holds back."

"I guess that part of our relationship wasn't meant to be. It's hard, but the more I've gotten to know Ben, the more it makes sense."

Anthony put his arm around Mike. "You know it was never just about HIV. All the safer sex education makes it seem like all of our problems would be solved with condoms. It's never just about condoms. It's about intimacy, the scary stuff that every loving relationship struggles with. Gay men just have the added burden of closets and shame and this damned disease. We don't give ourselves enough credit for the up-hill challenge. It's such a gift that you didn't run away. Thank you."

Mike sniffled. "I do love him. I could have made a life with him."

Judy put her hand on Mike's shoulder. "We all have some of that with Ben."

I scratched the back door. The rain was coming down faster. I wanted to run around in wet grass and feel the tickle of rain dripping from my nose.

Judy looked over at me. "Beau, you don't want to go out there. It's nasty outside."

"He doesn't care." Anthony sat down on the floor. "Come here, Beau." I ran and jumped into his lap. "Now, here's a creature that doesn't spend much time with disappointment. He makes the best of it, rain or shine."

"What are we going to do about Beau?" Mike asked. "He could stay with me and Farrah."

I perked up my ears.

"Thanks, that's sweet, but we have to find a way so he can stay here," Anthony replied.

Judy reached down and caressed the top of my head. "He's the best medicine Ben has." A drop of water rolled off her chin and landed on the floor. "It's one of the reasons Ben wants to be home."

Anthony sighed. "It's painful and beautiful to watch their relationship."

"I don't mind saying it—Beau's his great love." Judy picked me up out of Anthony's lap and put her head next to mine. "You're such an angel. I hope you know how much he loves you."

"I can help with dog walks," Mike said and then looked away. "What's going to happen . . . I mean when Ben's gone?"

Judy smiled sadly. "I guess Ben's finally going to get his wish. Anthony and I have to get along. We're Beau's godparents and we're going to share him. He's going to live part time with Anthony and part time with me."

White-shoes stood in the doorway. "Judy and Anthony, he's asking for you."

"I think I'm going to take off. I need to get ready for work." Mike stood up. "Let me know what shifts you want me to take."

"Thanks Mike, I'll give you a call," Anthony said.

Mike gave Judy and Anthony a hug. "Talk to you soon."

SEVERAL DAYS floated by like leaves without any place to land. The air in the house was stuffy and stale. Everyone walked around like they were looking for something but not with the excitement of a missing ball. They acted like they didn't expect to find what they were looking for. I didn't know how to play that game. The only place I felt right was outside. I loved my walks, where the air still smelled like the way things used to be. Rain was part of almost every walk. Water rushed down the hills and piled up at corners in great puddles, bringing with it all the treats and surprises that were waiting on sidewalks and streets. Anthony always made me walk around the adventure. I remember the times my dad let me splash right through.

On one wild windy and rainy day, Grandpa and Shirley arrived. They sat with Judy and Anthony in the sitting-room, staring at anything but each other. My hair was still damp after Anthony's attempt to dry me. Grandpa sat with a hard face. Shirley sat with tight lips. I ran from leg to leg trying to find a hand.

"Some weather you're having. A lady on the plane said it's El Nino. I thought it was supposed to be sunny in California," Shirley said with a forced smile.

"I want to talk to the doctor," Grandpa announced. Shirley reached over and held his hand.

"Sure, I'll give you his number," Anthony replied. "But maybe you want to see Ben first. He's in the bedroom."

"Of course," Shirley answered. "Is he awake?"

"He sleeps most of the time. If you want to call it sleep. He's having a hard time breathing. He's on oxygen. He's getting pain meds to try and make him comfortable."

"Don't they have new medicine for this now?" Grandpa asked. "I heard that Magic Johnson was cured."

"No one is cured," Anthony replied. "The media always gets it wrong. There are better medicines to control the virus but nothing to get rid of it."

"So what about Ben?" Grandpa continued. "Can't he get some of that medicine?"

"They didn't work so well for Ben." Anthony looked away. "He had lots of side effects so he stopped taking them."

"This is too much. My son is dying, and this is the first I hear that he's sick. Why didn't someone tell me?" Grandpa looked at Anthony and Judy.

"You mean why didn't Ben tell you?" Anthony's tone was stern.

Judy raised her hand toward Anthony and turned to Grandpa. "Harvey, you know Ben. He tries to deal with everything alone. It took a long time for him to tell me."

Anthony turned toward Grandpa. "Maybe he didn't tell because he didn't want to deal with the fallout."

Grandpa's eyes narrowed. "What fallout? What are you saying?"

Judy interrupted again. "Just that he was scared. He was scared that those he loved wouldn't love him if they knew."

"Poor boy. All alone with this." Shirley dabbed her eyes with a cloth. "He just needs our love, dear."

"I want to talk to the doctor," Grandpa said again.

MORE DAYS TRUDGED on, as the house seemed to change. My dad was drifting further away from the familiar places we used to share. I was curled up on the eating-room floor, watching Judy and Anthony. They sat across from each other at the table with cups in front of them.

"It's getting harder and harder for him to breathe," Anthony said softly into his cup.

Judy bowed her head. "He's not even drinking."

They sat in silence, staring down at the wisps of steam floating up from their cups.

Anthony slowly raised his head and looked at Judy, "He's going to leave soon." Anthony's shoulders started to shake.

Judy reached across the table and held Anthony's hand and whimpered. "I know." She took a shaky breath. "How is it possible? I can't imagine it . . . life without him. He always said that love and pain went together. I thought he was a pessimist, but maybe he's right."

"Don't you hate it when he's right?" Anthony smiled a crooked smile.

Judy sniffled. "Yes. I would give anything for one more fight with him. They seem precious now. Isn't that messed up?"

"No, I always knew that you two fought because you loved each other. You had the kind of love that just didn't know where to go."

Judy wiped her eyes. "Did he ever give you that line that love always involves good-bye?"

"Yeah, I thought he was jaded. He said every relationship ends; either someone leaves or someone dies."

Judy shook her head. "But he used it as a reason to be miserly and cautious. You know what? If I had the chance, I would do it all over again, pain and all." Judy gave a sad chuckle. "The little shit, I sure hope he left me lots of money for therapy."

Anthony laughed from his belly. It was an Anthony laugh that filled a room and made everyone smile. My tail sprung into action. I danced over to Anthony to the sweet sounds of play. Judy started to giggle. Every time one of them slowed, the other one started up again with snorts and fits of happy. I raced around the room and did summersaults. Then just as suddenly as the fun had entered the room, it left. Judy and Anthony sat at the table with tears rolling down their faces.

# Chapter 22

## Good-Bye

The air was heavy with waiting. The voices in the room were hushed and low. Dim lights cast strange shadows, making the humans look like they were floating. I panted, uneasy, rough pink tongue dripping and dangling from my black lips. My dad's hand rested limp on my head without any petting. In between coughs, his body lay motionless. I wasn't sleepy. Something unknown was waiting in the room.

I was in HIS bed! So many times I had tried to land in his bed, a high jump that always ended with a scolding and a push to the floor. My dad always loved his bed. I wanted to love it, too. But it was one of the places I wasn't welcomed.

And yet, there I was, next to him in his soft and private place. Judy and Anthony had insisted. I was sure my dad would open his eyes at any moment and chase me off. I lay there tense and alert. He was attached to a web of tubes. One was stuck in his arm and attached to a bag that hung overhead, another came out from under the blankets and ended in a yellow pouch, and one hung around his neck and ended in his nose. He sucked in each breath with loud stops and starts as a machine next to the bed hissed and pumped. His body smelled stale and sour.

"I'm not ready," Judy whispered between sniffles. Tears traveled down her cheeks, leaving dark trails. Her painted face held bloodshot eyes. She blew her nose and then turned to Anthony and lowered her voice further. "What should we do?"

Anthony's shoulders sagged. His muscular body, usually bouncing and erect, hung stooped and low. "Nothing."

Judy cried softly. "That's . . . that's not good enough." She ran her hand through my dad's hair, "I always want more than you can give."

My dad sucked in an extra long and hard breath and blew out something foul. I sniffed and nudged him with my nose. He groaned but didn't open his eyes. Judy and Anthony watched us in silence.

Anthony finally said, "Judy, he's suffering."

They both closed their eyes and with wrinkled faces started to cry. Humans are really much easier to understand when they don't use their words. I wagged my tail and started to get up so I could nuzzle them.

Anthony held me back by petting my thigh. "No, Beau." A tear rolled off his chin. "You stay . . . stay where you are."

Their sobs slowed as Grandpa's shadow entered the room and stood some distance from the bed. He sounded tired. "He could still get better. We're not going to just give up . . . are we?" The words hung in the air. No one answered. "He should be in a hospital."

Anthony shook his head and mumbled, "It's not what he wants."

White-shoes moved over to Grandpa and put her hand on his shoulder. "I know it's really hard, but I think your son is trying to make his transition."

Grandpa looked away and he wiped his sleeve across his face. "He's only thirty-five."

White-shoes sighed. "I know. It's way too soon."

Judy held out her hand toward Grandpa. "Come here, Harvey."

Grandpa shook his head. He walked out of the room and White-shoes followed.

My dad's eyes slowly half-opened. He moved his mouth, but only raspy air came out.

"What is it, Ben?" Anthony bent lower with his face next to my dad's.

My dad took a ragged breath. The coughs were sharp and brittle and he winced in pain. Judy and Anthony watched without breathing, waiting for the cough to ease. And then, as suddenly as he appeared, my dad closed his eyes and disappeared into his difficult sleep. Judy and Anthony stared at his chest as it moved up and down and air struggled in and out.

Judy's puffy eyes again filled with water and her lips quivered. "Soon," she said in a small voice.

Anthony nodded his head.

Judy closed her eyes as tears ran out their corners. "Our dear sweet Ben," she whispered.

Anthony and Judy looked at each other without words and then climbed into the bed, one on each side. They cuddled next to us and put their arms around my dad and me. I scooted up to Judy and put my nose next to her nose. Judy buried her face in my hair with her snot and tears. Lazy music hummed quietly, somewhere in the room a tick-tock ticked without missing a beat, the machine next to the bed whooshed in and out like sleepy-time snores, and my dad's breathing struggled to keep up. His eyelashes fluttered like tiny butterfly wings. Anthony and Judy cried softly. I whined. We all waited with whimpers and breaths.

# Chapter 23

## Fly

Farrah and I raced down the sandy steps to get to the bottom. The humans took their time. There was glittering sand as far as I could see, soft and warm and then hard and cool near the water-that-never-ends. Great mounds of water crashed and then rolled back, leaving puddles of white foam. It was my dad's favorite place. It was always familiar and always different. Sometimes the water was gray and brown, wild and angry, sometimes blue and green, friendly and gentle. It could change in a moment, at times playing nice and then knocking me over and sending me tumbling. Sometimes slimy plants and water creatures were everywhere, and sometimes the sand was washed clean and white. This day it was wide and empty, except for us.

Anthony, Judy, Mrs. Harris, Mike, Grandpa, and Shirley slowly made their way toward us. Anthony and Judy had their pant legs rolled up and were barefoot. Farrah and I were already wet, sandy, and salty.

"It's his kind of day." Anthony breathed deeply.

"Sure is, all this sun, he must be smiling," Mike added.

Mrs. Harris was walking carefully and holding Mike's arm. "Perfect," she said.

Judy carried a colorful jar. "I expect to turn around and see him throwing Beau's ball. You know, it was Beau's birthday last month, two-years-old."

Anthony smiled. "Remember when Ben first got Beau? He was so excited. I think it was his way of choosing to live." Anthony wiped his eyes with his sleeve. "I just can't hold on to it . . . that he's gone."

After that night when strangers put my dad in a bag and took him away, his scent had grown faint. I spent days looking for him. Even the things that reminded me of him became fuzzy without his smell. He was gone. Every day took me further from where I used to be. And then I was taken away. My new home was with Judy some days and then with Anthony the other days. I had pillows and toys at each house. Only my food bowl traveled with me wherever I went, the same shiny bowl that had held every meal my dad had ever given me.

Anthony continued, "I was watching a mom at the park play peek-a-boo with her kid. I wanted to warn the kid that it's a setup — sometimes, they really don't come back."

"He never wanted to play with me." Grandpa's voice was husky and hoarse. "He always preferred his mother."

Shirley handed Grandpa a small cloth, but he pushed her hand away.

I ran circles around Anthony. He reached into his pocket and pulled out my new bouncy ball. He threw it high and far. I chased the ball and Farrah chased me. When I caught up with the ball, it tasted like it had been swimming with the fishes. I brought it back and dropped it at Anthony's feet.

"I still can't believe he went so fast." Mike shook his head. "I thought there would be more time."

"Maybe it was a blessing. He didn't suffer very long." Shirley said.

Anthony and Judy looked at each other and nodded.

Grandpa shook his head. "He should've told me."

"He did the best he could." Shirley held on to Grandpa's elbow.

"It was what it was." Anthony picked up my ball and looked into the sun. He took a deep breath and turned to Grandpa. "Harvey, do you know how courageous your son was? Do you know the guts it takes a gay man to tell the world that he's gay? Do you know the guts it takes to live with a disease that most of society thinks is dirty and a consequence of sin? Do you know the guts it takes to live when every day something reminds you of a disease that will probably take your life? You should be proud of him."

Grandpa stared out at the water.

"We are proud of him." Shirley held Grandpa's arm tighter.

"But it never hurts to say it." Anthony threw my ball.

"We never say it enough to those we love," Mrs. Harris smiled sadly. "None of us."

When I returned with the ball, the humans were standing in a row on the dry, warm sand, just out of reach of the water rolling in and out.

"Who wants to go first?" Judy held up the jar.

"I will." Mike reached for the jar. Judy lifted the lid and Mike grabbed something from inside. "Thank you, Ben. Thank you for all those special times. They were delicious times. Can I just say, that man could cook!" Everyone smiled and nodded their heads. "I know it was hard to open your heart, but I'm glad that you let me have a peek." He threw something in the air. It blew away in the wind like sand. Mike's shoulders started to shake, and something like a moan came from deep in his throat.

Anthony put his arm around Mike. "He did have a beautiful heart. I don't think he understood his own beauty, but we saw it." Anthony looked at the jar. "Ben, I miss you so much. I can't tell you how many times I pick up the phone to dial your number. I hope you're basking in love wherever you are and that you're getting some action." He chuckled through his tears. "Actually, I hope you're getting a lot." He put his hand in the jar and pulled out a handful. "I wish you could still be here." He bit his lower lip and paused. "But since you can't . . . go ahead and fly." He tossed the grey powder, and they all watched it float away.

Shirley nudged Grandpa. He shifted from one foot to the other. Judy handed the jar to Grandpa, but he didn't take it. Shirley put her hand in the jar and took out a handful and sprinkled it slowly in the sand. "We love you," she said with tears.

Judy hugged the jar. "This is not Ben, but it's all we have left." Judy reached into the jar and started to cry. "How can this be?" Her voice was wobbly. "I'll always love you, you impossible and beautiful man. I hope you are finally in a place where you can know love. Love big, love without fear, but mostly let yourself be loved." She raised her fist and opened her fingers. Tiny specks flew away.

They all stood in silence and stared out into the water. After much waiting and no ball throwing, I barked. Anthony looked down at me and then turned to Mrs. Harris. "Could you say a prayer?"

Mrs. Harris nodded. Her brown face was streaked with two faint white trails from her eyes to her chin. She lowered her head and cleared her throat. "Heavenly Father," she said slowly and then paused. "At times like these I don't know how to pray." Mrs. Harris pulled out a white cloth and blew her nose. "But in the confusion and pain of death I want to give thanks for your creation." I ran over to Mrs. Harris and tried to put my nose in her pocket. She smiled. "Yes, *all* of your special creation." She patted my head. "Lord, you have called us by name at the moment of our birth. Yet despite all you have given us, we often fall short of that birthright. Forgive us when we demean and judge your creation. Forgive us when we forget our names and allow others to name us. Today we remember and celebrate Ben. Thank you for his life and the lessons we learned from witnessing his journey. May we live with a renewed commitment to love as you loved him, with more forgiveness, more understanding, and more grace. We commend Ben's spirit to the everlasting arms of his Creator, knowing he is home. Amen."

Everyone was crying. Off in the distance I saw it coming . . . a big wave was growing and moving towards the shore.

Mike saw it first and shouted, "RUN. Here comes a big one!"

All of a sudden the big swell of water rushed towards us, covering everyone's feet in wetness. All the humans started to run for dry ground. At the same time a wild wind blew in from nowhere, this way and that. As Judy ran, the jar slipped in her arms and tipped. The wind caught some of the powder and blew it in all directions. They all shouted, waved their arms, and stomped their feet. Then just as suddenly something changed, like unexpected sunshine after a rain. Anthony and Judy stopped running and started to laugh. They looked at each other, shoulders shaking, with red-eyes and puffy faces. Judy smiled a crooked smile and reached into the jar. She pulled out her hand and dropped the jar in the sand. With her clenched fist in the air, she ran towards the water-that-never-ends. Anthony and I raced after her. Judy released the last handful of powder and we splashed in the icy cold and danced among the swirling flakes.

I'M ALWAYS losing things. And it's always the things I love the most that end up missing. I still sometimes look for him. Sometimes I even think I see him. Luckily, I have more than my eyes to help me find my way. The good thing about living on all fours is that my nose is always close to the right stuff. It's down here where I can figure out the difference between a wish and a whiff. A wish is when I look for things after the sniff trail has gone cold, but a whiff is when I look for something that has real possibility. Nothing is as exciting as finding a new adventure. It doesn't really matter how it turns out. It's the excitement of finding it that makes my stub tail wag. I hope that wherever my dad is, that he is on his hands and knees with his nose to the ground and that his tail is wagging. Life is best lived when you can really smell it.

# About the Author

Author, advocate, and psychotherapist, David Fredrickson has dedicated his professional life to the psychosocial needs of underserved communities including at-risk children, adolescents, and families and those affected by HIV/AIDS.

Currently, David lends his mental health expertise to non-profits. He is on the board of directors of the HIV Story Project—a non-profit focused on bridging HIV/AIDS with film, media and storytelling. He also facilitates peer support groups addressing the needs of the LGBT community at the University of California, San Francisco, Alliance Health Project.

David grew up in the Midwest where faith, family, and food were the bedrock of his childhood. A long-time resident of San Francisco, David attends GLIDE Memorial Church and sings with its world-renowned GLIDE Ensemble. His family has multiplied into a village and they are often found in his kitchen consuming sweet and savory miracles.

David's next project is a collection of short stories about Swedish immigration, migration, four generations of family, and identity within an evolving American society.

Contact David at www.davidafredickson.com.

Made in the USA
Charleston, SC
18 December 2014